哈福

哈福

英文流利・談笑風生

★★★★★★★★★★★★★★★★★★★★★★★★★★ 施孝昌◎著

跟老外

Making Friends in English

交友學英語

哈福

英文流利，和老外談笑風生

碰到老外大膽開口說

英語是全地球的語言！您必定知道，不論是您個人的事業前途，企業的擴張，還是學習、知識的增進，都必須會說英語。

於是，您在多年以前就開始認字母、背單字、記文法，接受一系列的英文大考小考。

但截至現在，您在英文上所下的功夫，已經可以幫您光大個人事業、拓展企業、獲取最新知識了嗎？您自認為您現在「會說」英語了嗎？

日本在國際上最成功的的公司—SONY電器的總裁，盛田昭夫先生本身在國際上也很著名，因為他能說一口流利的英語。他的學習英語之道，用他自己的話解釋是：「將通用的英語，親身去實際應用，就是學英語之道了。」

反過來看您學的英語，是「通用的英語」嗎？還是艱澀的文章？甚至是錯誤百出的洋涇濱？

要怎樣才能「親身實際應用」通用的英語呢？

最有效的方法就是「交朋友」，交很多老外朋友！

但碰到老外如何開場白？如何自我介紹？這也是一門學問。

朋友的交往是靠溝通的；在與老外交往時，您可以藉著親身溝通機會學到很多常用的英語，在溝通應用中，自然就會說流利的英語了。

目前，不論您是走在本國的街頭，或是在外國旅遊觀光、遊學移民，結交外國朋友的機會多得很，問題是，您可以先開口用英語去結交朋友（make friends）嗎？別忘了，朋友是靠「製造」（make）得來的。

本書的目的，就是要讓您敢主 先向外國人開口說英語！

本書的內容包括所有人與人交往時，一定會談到的英語短句、成語、會話、單字。涵蓋了所有生活、休閒、社交、商務等話題，都是每天必用的英語會話。

本書全部是最純正的英語。不用再死背艱深的單字，卻最能生動、明白地將意思表達出來。

本書的編排方式，每句對話都註明是「中國人」或「外國人」。在自己的國家與老外交往時，您的角色是中國人，對方是外國人；到了國外交友，您就成了外國人，所以書中的每一句話，您都用得上。

書中每課都有「進階應用」會話，每個對話都標有使用場合和時機。重要語句全部挑出標色，讓您更能自然熟記應用。

熟讀本書的內容，熟聽MP3裡實際對話的語調，您就能徹底突破學習英語的瓶頸，在各種場合，與老外談笑風生！

Chapter 6 商業友誼英語

Chapter 7 關懷朋友英語

本書的目的：

讓您敢主動先向外國人開口說英語！
熟讀本書內容，熟聽MP3，就能說一
口流利的英語！

Chapter 1

建立友誼英語

用英語自我介紹

Is this your first time in Taiwan?
這是你第一次到台灣嗎？

精華短句 一學就會！最簡單、迷你的會話

- How are you doing?
  （你好嗎？）

- Glad to meet you.
  （很高興認識你。）

- Is this your first time in Taiwan?
  （這是你第一次到台灣嗎？）

- Here is my phone number.
  （這是我的電話號碼。）

- I would like that.
  （我會需要的。）

- Where are you from?
  （你從那裡來？）

- Are you here on vacation or business?
  （你是來這裡度假還是談生意？）

- Do you speak any English?
  （你會說英文嗎？）
- Where did you learn Chinese?
  （你在那裡學會中文？）

實況會話 靈活運用！會話、聽力同步加強

中：	Good afternoon!	午安！
外：	Hi, how are you doing?	嗨，你好嗎？
中：	Fine, thanks. I am Robert.	很好，謝謝。 我是羅勃。
外：	Glad to meet you, Robert. I am Mary.	很高興見到你，羅勃。我是瑪麗。
中：	Is this your first time in Taiwan?	這是你第一次到台灣嗎？
外：	Yes. My company has an office here, and I have just been transferred.	是的。 我們公司在這裡有個辦事處，我是剛剛才調過來的。

中：	Here is my phone number. If you need anyone to show you around, call me.	這是我的電話號碼。 如果你需要人帶你四處逛逛，可以打電話給我。
外：	Great. I would like that.	太棒了。 我會需要的。

進階應用 舉一反三！聽說力更上一層樓

⊃ 問人家從哪裡來，怎麼說？

中： Where are you from?
你從哪裡來？

外： I am from Texas, but I have lived in Taiwan for the last three months.
我從德州來，但是最近三個月都住在台灣。

⊃ 自願帶外國朋友到餐館，怎麼說？

外： Excuse me, where is the closest place to eat?
對不起，最近可以吃東西的地方在哪裡？

中： Down the street about four blocks.
沿著這條街下去大約過四條街口。

I can take you there if you like.
如果你需要，我可以帶你去。

⊃ 與外國朋友初見面

中： Hi, I am Robert.
嗨，我是羅勃。

Are you here on vacation or business?
你是來這裡渡假還是談生意？

外： I am here on vacation.
我來這裡渡假。

I think Taiwan is beautiful!
台灣是個漂亮的地方！

⊃ 問是否會說中文，怎麼說？

中： Do you speak any Chinese?
你會說中文嗎？

外： No, I do not, but I am trying to learn.
不，我不會，但我想學。

Where did you learn English?
你的英文是在哪裡學的？

　　英語談到地理位置，經常用到block這個字，中文沒有直接相對應的說法，因為我們的都市計畫沒有做那麼整齊，它指的是，都市裡東西南北四條街圍起來的一個區段。

　　注意英語的Where are you from?不一定是問「你從哪裡來？」，特別是在初見面的英語會話中，假如聽到這一句，那對方一定是在問你是哪一國人，你應該以國名或大地名回答。如I am from Taiwan.；I am from Japan.。

　　I would like that.表示你很同意對方的提議。當對方表達了願意幫忙的意願時，你可以說Thank you. I would like that.（謝謝，感謝你的好意。）

每課一句 3秒鐘，強化英語力！

🔊 I am just now learning English.
（我現在才剛在學英文。）

🔊 I know only a little English.
（我只懂一點英文。）

🔊 I would like to have someone to practice my English with.
（我想找一個人來練習英文。）

常用單字 3秒鐘，強化單字力！

afternoon [ˌæftɚˈnun]	下午
glad [glæd]	高興
fine [faɪn]	好的
company [ˈkʌmpənɪ]	公司
office [ˈɔfɪs]	辦公室
transfer [ˈtrænsfɚ]	調職
show ~ around	帶某人四處逛逛
closest	最接近的
vacation [vəˈkeʃən]	假期
business [ˈbɪzənəs]	商務
beautiful [ˈbjutəfəl]	漂亮
learn [lɝn]	學習
practice [ˈpræktɪs]	練習

🔊 Pursuits become habits.
（因循會變成習慣。）

用英語介紹朋友

This is my friend Mike.
這是我的朋友麥克。

精華短句 一學就會！最簡單、迷你的會話

- Excuse me.
  （對不起。）

- I am a little lost.
  （我有點迷路了）

- Which way is downtown?
  （到市區要走那一條路？）

- Good to meet you.
  （很愉快能認識你。）

- Pretty easy to tell.
  （很容易就看得出來。）

- Not really.
  （不見得。）

- We do not see many Americans.
  （我們很少見到美國人。）

- We are happy to help.
  （我們很樂意幫忙。）
- Have you met my friend Mike?
  （你見過我的朋友麥克了嗎？）

實況會話 靈活運用！會話、聽力同步加強

外：	Excuse me, I am a little lost. Which way is downtown?	對不起，我有點迷路了。 到市區要怎麼走？
中：	It is to your left. By the way, I am Robert, and this is my friend Mike.	往你的左手邊走。 對了，我是羅勃，這是我的朋友麥克。
外：	Good to meet you.	很高興見到你。
中：	Is this your first time in Taipei?	這是你第一次到台北嗎？
外：	Yes. Pretty easy to tell, huh?	是的。 很容易就看得出來，是嗎？

15

中：	No, not really. We do not see many Americans.	不，不見得。 我們很少見到美國人。
外：	Actually, I am Canadian.	事實上，我是加拿大人。
中：	Oh. Well, if you need a tour of the city, we are happy to help.	噢。 嗯，如果你要遊覽本市，我們很樂意幫忙。

進階應用 舉一反三！聽說力更上一層樓

⊃ 介紹外國新朋友，怎麼說？

外： Have you met my friend Mike?
你見過我的朋友麥克嗎？

中： No.
沒有。

Hi, Mike!
嗨，麥克！

⊃ 初見外國朋友

外： This is my friend Mike.
這是我的朋友麥克。

He is from Hong Kong.
他從香港來。

中： **Hello, Mike.**
嗨，麥克。

Have you been in Taipei long?
你在台北很久了嗎？

⊃ 已有一面之緣的說法

外： **Do you know Mike?**
你認識麥克嗎？

中： **Yes, I think we met last week.**
是的，我想我們上個禮拜見過面。

⊃ 詢問名字，怎麼說？

中： **I am sorry, but I don't know your name.**
對不起，我不知道你的名字。

外： **I am Mary.**
我是瑪麗。

中： **I am Robert, and this is my friend Mike.**
我是羅勃，這是我的朋友麥克。

外： **It is nice to meet you.**
很高興能認識你們。

　　本unit學習如何介紹自己和同行的人。注意介紹同行的人給對方認識時，英語要用「This is + 人名」的句型，說話的同時，五指併攏指著被介紹的人；千萬不要用一根指頭指人，也不可用「He is ……」或「She is ……」，兩樣都非常不禮貌。

　　Pretty easy to tell.的tell不是「說」的意思，而是「分辨」。天天用的英語會話經常用到這種用法，例如：Can you tell which one is yours?（你看得出來哪個是你的嗎？）

　　注意英語談到國籍時，一般不加冠詞，I am Chinese.指的是「我是中國人。」。你有時也可以說I am a Chinese. I love my country.（我是一個中國人，我愛我的國家。）這時，在Chinese之前加冠詞a，是強調我是中國的「一份子」，與國籍無關。

每課一句 3秒鐘，強化英語力！

◀ Where are you from?
（你是哪裡人？）

◀ Where do you come from?
（你從哪裡來？）

◀ Are you from America?
（你是美國來的嗎？）

◀ Are you American?
（你是美國人嗎？）

常用單字 3秒鐘，強化單字力！

lost [lɔst]
遺失

downtown [ˈdaʊnˈtaʊn]
市區

meet [mit]
見面

pretty [ˈprɪtɪ]
漂亮

friend [frɛnd]
朋友

Canadian [kəˈnedɪən]
加拿大人

🔊 When sorrow is asleep, wake it not.
（傷心舊事別重提。）

19

用英語打招呼

How are you doing today?
你今天好嗎？

精華短句 一學就會！最簡單、迷你的會話

- I am fine.
  （我很好。）

- That would be great.
  （那樣可太好了。）

- Me, too.
  （我也是。）

- Where would you like to go?
  （你想去哪裡？）

- Are you waiting for the bus?
  （你在等公車嗎？）

- I do not think we have met before.
  （我想我們以前沒見過。）

- How are you today?
  （你今天好嗎？）

- What about yourself?
  （那麼你自己如何呢？）

實況會話 靈活運用！會話、聽力同步加強

外：	Hi. How are you doing today?	嗨。 你今天好嗎？
中：	I am O.K. What about you?	我還不錯。 那麼你呢？
外：	I am fine, thanks.	我很好，謝謝。
中：	Do you have any plans for the afternoon?	下午你有什麼計劃嗎？
外：	Not really, but I need to eat lunch soon.	還沒有，但是我等一下要吃午餐。
中：	Me, too. Do you want to grab a bite to eat?	我也是。 你想要一起吃點東西嗎？

外：	That would be great. Where would you like to go?	那太好了。你想去哪裡吃呢？
中：	Wherever you think the best food is.	你想那裡有最好的食物，我們就去。

進階應用 舉一反三！聽說力更上一層樓

⟲ 早上見面寒喧

中： Good Morning.
早安。

Are you waiting for the bus?
你在等公車嗎？

外： Yes, I am going downtown.
是的，我要去市區。

⟲ 第一次見面打招呼

中： Hi.
嗨。

I do not think we have met before.
我想我們以前沒見過吧。

I am Robert.
我是羅勃。

外： Nice to meet you, Robert. I am Mary.
很高興認識你，羅勃，我是瑪麗。

つ 每日見面問候

中： How are you today?
你今天好嗎？

外： I am fine.
我很好。

What about yourself?
那你自己呢？

つ 下午見到女士的問候法

中： Good afternoon, madam. How are you
today?
午安，女士，你今天好嗎？

外： I am O.K.
我還好。

But I am tired of waiting for the bus!
但我等公車等得很煩了。

純英語句型解說

　　學習英語或英語，一定要以純正為原則，千萬不要講洋涇濱英文，所以要有一本好的教材，跟著學習，不要養成隨便編造的習慣。在本書中你會經常看到「Do you have any plans +時間？」，這就是一句標準英語句型，它與plan的原意「計畫」沒多大關係，意思是「你是否已經約了人在某個時間一起吃飯或做其他活動？」，講這句話，八成是要提出某種邀請，事先探一下時間有沒有衝突。

　　grab a bite to eat直譯是「抓一口來吃」，問人家要不要grab a bite，就是提議一起去「隨便吃點飯」，不但有邀請的意思，還有「不要花太多錢」的含意。

　　下面的「每課一句」中要學一句Is this a busy afternoon, or what?這種「Is ……, or what?」的句型，很重要，它的外表看起來是個疑問句的樣子，有個大問號在，但其實說話的人是在「感嘆」，表示有些「無奈」或「不能置信」的感嘆。例如：Are you crazy, or what? (你瘋啦！怎麼會做出這種事來？)

每課一句　3秒鐘，強化英語力！

◀» Is this seat taken?
　（這個座位有人坐嗎？）

◀» Do you mind if I sit next to you?
　（如果我坐在你旁邊，你介意嗎？）

◀» Is this a busy afternoon, or what?
　（今天下午怎麼搞的，這麼忙。）

常用單字 3秒鐘，強化單字力！

plan [plæn]
計劃

really [ˈriəlɪ]
真的

grab
抓

bite [baɪt]
一口

wherever
任何一個地方

wait
等待

madam [ˈmædəm]
女士

tired of
厭倦

🔊 Obedience is the first duty of a soldier.
（軍人以服從為天職。）

🔊 Public before private and country before family.
（先公而後私，先國而後家。）

用英語搭訕─談天氣

I heard it was going to rain!
我聽說快要下雨了！

精華短句 一學就會！最簡單、迷你的會話

- Nice afternoon, isn't it?
  （下午天氣真好，不是嗎？）

- Who knows?
  （天曉得！）

- It is so unpredictable.
  （天氣真是不可預測。）

- Do you think it will rain?
  （你想會不會下雨？）

- Beautiful sunset, isn't it?
  （落日很漂亮，不是嗎？）

- I had not noticed.
  （我沒有注意到。）

- We do need it.
  （我們真的很需要。）

- Nice weather we are having.
  （天氣真棒。）

實況會話 靈活運用！會話、聽力同步加強

中：	Nice afternoon, isn't it?	下午天氣好棒，不是嗎？
外：	Oh, yes. Beautiful weather.	噢，是啊！ 天氣很好。
中：	I think it is supposed to get hot later in the week.	我想這星期稍後的天氣應該會變熱。
外：	Really? I heard it was going to rain!	真的嗎？我聽說快要下雨了！
中：	Well, it's weather. Who knows?	唉呀，天氣就是天氣。 誰知道會怎樣？

外：	Really. It is so unpredictable.	是啊。 天氣真是難以預測。
中：	By the way, I am Robert.	對了，我是羅勃。
外：	Oh, hi Robert. I am Mary.	噢，嗨，羅勃。 我叫瑪麗。

進階應用 舉一反三！聽說力更上一層樓

⊃ 表示希望不要下雨

中： Do you think it will rain?
你想會下雨嗎？

外： It might.
有可能。

Hopefully not before the bus comes!
希望在公車來之前，不要下！

⊃ 表示未注意，怎麼說？

中： Good evening.
晚安。

Beautiful sunset, isn't it?
晚霞很美，不是嗎？

外： I had not noticed...
我沒有注意到……。

You are right. It is pretty.
你說得對，它是很美。

⊃ **表示不敢相信會下雨，怎麼說？**

中： Hi.
嗨。

Can you believe this rain?
你能相信下這樣的雨嗎？

外： Well, we do need it.
嗯，我們真的需要。

The ground has been dry.
地面一直很乾。

⊃ **談論好天氣**

中： Nice weather we are having.
天氣很好啊。

外： Yes.
是的。

Is the weather always this nice in Taiwan?
台灣的天氣都是這麼好嗎？

Who knows?的英語說法，在表面上也是問句，其實，它只是一句隨口而出的話，意思是「天曉得！」，無人可以預知。

Nice weather we are having.在英文法上稱為「倒裝句」，原來的句子是We are having nice weather.，說話時，為了強調nice weather（好天氣），所以把nice weather調到句子最前面。

每課一句 3秒鐘，強化英語力！

📢 I think a storm is coming.
（我想暴風雨快來了。）

📢 Do you know if it is going to rain tomorrow?
（你知道明天會不會下雨？）

📢 It sure is hot today, isn't it?
（今天真的很熱，對不？）

📢 Do you mind if I grab this seat next to you?
（我坐你旁邊的座位，不介意吧？）

📢 Be swift to hear slow to speak.
（敏捷的聽，緩慢的說。）

常用單字 3秒鐘，強化單字力！

nice
好的

supposed to
料想會

unpredictable
[ˌʌnprɪˈdɪktəbḷ]
不可預測

by the way
對了；順便一提

hopefully [ˈhopfəlɪ]
希望

sunset [ˈsʌnˌsɛt]
落日；晚霞

notice [ˈnotɪs]
注意

ground [graʊnd]
地面

dry
乾的

storm
暴風雨

🔊 The voice of the people is the voice of God.
（人民的聲音就是上帝的聲音。）

用英語搭訕―談穿著

That is a nice tie.
那條領帶很棒

 06

精華短句　一學就會！最簡單、迷你的會話

- I got it in America.
  （我在美國買的。）

- Do you live in Taipei?
  （你住在台北嗎？）

- I live just outside of the city.
  （我住在市郊。）

- I really like your shoes.
  （我真的喜歡你的鞋子。）

- Where did you get your dress for the party?
  （你在那裡買到舞會穿的洋裝？）

- What is that logo on your hat?
  （你帽子上是什麼標誌？）

- Do you think this shirt looks okay on me?
  （你覺得這件襯衫我穿起來還可以嗎？）

實況會話 靈活運用！會話、聽力同步加強

中：	Nice shirt. Do you mind if I ask where you got it?	好棒的襯衫。 你介意我問你，你是在哪裡買的嗎？
外：	I got it in America.	我在美國買的。
中：	Is that where you are from?	你就是從美國來的嗎？
外：	Yes, I am here with my company. We have an office in Taipei.	是的，我是來此地上班。 我們公司在台北有辦公室。
中：	Wow. Oh, by the way, my name is Robert.	噢。 啊，對了，我的名字是羅勃。
外：	I am Mary. Do you live in Taipei?	我是瑪麗。 你住在台北嗎？
中：	No, I live just outside of the city.	不，我住在台北郊區。
外：	I am not real familiar with the area.	這一帶我還不是很熟。

⊃ 讚美他人的穿著

中： I really like your shoes!
我真的很喜歡你的鞋子!

外： Oh, thank you.
噢，謝謝。

I just bought them today.
我今天剛買的。

⊃ 詢問衣服是從哪裏買的？

中： Where did you get your dress for the party?
你在那裡買到舞會穿的洋裝？

外： I brought it with me from America.
我從美國帶來的。

⊃ 讚美他人的服飾

外： That is a nice tie.
那條領帶很棒。

I have not seen another like it.
我沒有看過像這樣的領帶。

中： Thank you, it was a birthday gift.
謝謝你，這是別人送的生日禮物。

⊃ 詢問衣飾商標的問法？

中： What is that logo on your hat?
你帽上是什麼標誌？

外： It is a logo for an American baseball team called the Rangers.
這是叫「游騎兵」的美國棒球隊的商標。

純英語句型解說

秘密都在這裡！

　　本unit要學幾個介係詞的用法。介係詞是英語句型裡很重要的組成部份，但因為說英語時，介係詞往往沒有重音，輕輕一帶就過去了，所以很多學習英文的人，聽不清英美人士到底用那個字做介係詞，造成很多學習困擾。每個介係詞都有特別的意思，用錯介係詞，語意就會不清楚，所以要先看書，知道該用那個介係詞，再注意聽MP3裡老師的示範，多聽幾次，就能分辨每個介係詞的發音，知道到底哪個字是哪個字。

　　表示對某種東西很熟悉，用familiar with。

　　衣物是穿在身「上」，所以介係詞用on，例如：The shirt looks good on you.（這件襯衫你穿起來很好看。）「每課一句」裡的恭維的話：I really like what you have on.也是一樣的用法。

　　Do you live in Taipei? 的in指台北是個大都市。

🔊 Do you think this color looks okay on me?
（你覺得這個顏色合適我嗎？）

🔊 Where did you get your clothes?
（你在那裡買你的衣服？）

🔊 I really like what you have on.
（我真的喜歡你的穿著。）

🔊 I love your haircut.
（我喜歡你的髮型。）

🔊 Did you have it cut here in Taipei?
（你是在台北剪的嗎？）

shirt	襯衫
outside ['aʊt'saɪd]	外圍
familiar with	熟悉
bought [bɔt]	買（buy的過去式）
brought with	帶來（bring的過去式）
tie	領帶
birthday gift	生日禮物
logo ['logo]	標誌；商標
haircut ['hɛr,kʌt]	髮型

歡迎觀光客的英語

How do you like the city?
你還喜歡本市吧？

精華短句 一學就會！最簡單、迷你的會話

- Is this your first time in Taiwan?
  （這是你第一次到台灣嗎？）

- That would be nice.
  （那樣太好了。）

- Are you looking for something?
  （你在找什麼嗎？）

- I am just touring the city.
  （我是來這城市旅遊。）

- Have you been to Taipei before?
  （你以前到過台北嗎？）

- What is your accent?
  （你是那裡的口音？）

- How do you like the food here?
  （你還喜歡這裡的食物吧？）

- We will call you when we get settled in.
  （等我們安頓好之後，會打電話給你。）

實況會話 靈活運用！會話、聽力同步加強

中：	Good afternoon, is this your first time in Taiwan?	午安，這是你第一次到台灣嗎？
外：	Yes, it is.	是的，我是。
中：	Great. I am just learning English myself, but I love to meet Americans that I can practice with.	太好了。 我自己剛在學英文，但我喜歡認識美國人，練習英文。
外：	Well, it is a nice surprise to meet someone who does speak English.	原來如此。遇見會說英語的人，是個愉快的驚喜。
中：	If you would like, I can show you the high points of the city.	如果你喜歡，我可以帶你參觀本市主要的景點。

外：	That would be nice. We are staying at the Hyatt downtown.	那太好了。我們住在市區的凱悅飯店。
中：	I'll give you my number.	我給你我的電話號碼。
外：	We will call you when we get settled in.	等我們安頓好以後，我會打電話給你。

進階應用 舉一反三！聽說力更上一層樓

⊃ **藉題結交觀光客，怎麼說？**

中： Hi, are you looking for something?
　　嗨，你在找什麼嗎？

外： No, I am just touring the city.
　　不，我只是來這個城市觀光的。

　　Do you know of any good spots?
　　你知道那裡有好玩的觀光點？

⊃ **帶外國朋友到餐廳**

外： Excuse me, sir. I am looking for a place to eat.
　　先生，對不起，我正在找地方用餐。

中： Oh, I can show you one just down the street.
噢，我可以帶你到這條路下去不遠的一家館子。

Have you been in Taipei before?
你以前來過台北嗎？

⊃ 問外國訪客從那裡來

中： What is your accent? Are you from America, or Europe?
你是那裡的口音？你是美國人，還是歐洲人？

外： I am from France.
我來自法國。

純英語句型解說

秘密都在這裡！

　　「How do you like ……?」的句型，雖然用how起頭，但沒有其原意「如何」或「怎樣」的意思，而是問like（喜歡）到「什麼程度」？例如：How do you like the new job?（你對新工作還喜歡吧？）

　　It's a surprise.表示「好訝異」。英語若要表示好訝異，但「我很喜歡」這樣的訝異，只要在 surprise之前加上nice就行，整個句型就生動起來，有「驚喜」的意思了。

每課一句 3秒鐘,強化英語力!

📢 How do you like the place?
（你覺得這個地方如何？）

📢 Have you seen the major tourist attractions?
（你看過主要的觀光景點嗎？）

📢 I have always wanted to see America.
（我一直想要去美國看看。）

📢 How do you like the people here?
（你覺得這裡的人怎樣？）

📢 How long will you be vacationing here?
（你要在這裡渡假多久？）

常用單字 3秒鐘,強化單字力!

tour　[tʊr]	觀光
accent [ˈæksn̩t]	口音
major	主要
tourist [ˈtʊrɪst]	觀光客
attraction [əˈtrækʃən]	吸引
be settled in	安頓;適應

歡迎商務伙伴

It's nice to finally meet you in person.

很高興終於見到你本人。

精華短句 一學就會！最簡單、迷你的會話

- **How was your flight?**
  （你的飛行旅程如何？）

- **I will look forward to it.**
  （我會期待的。）

- **I am glad to see that you got here safely.**
  （我很高興看見你安全抵達這裡。）

- **How is the hotel?**
  （旅館還好嗎？）

- **Is this your first visit to Taiwan?**
  （這是你第一次訪問台灣嗎？）

◀》 Every man is his own worst enemy.
人生最大的敵人，就是自己。

實況會話 靈活運用！會話、聽力同步加強

中：	Good Morning. How was your flight?	早安。你的飛行旅程如何？
外：	Actually, I wish we had come a day earlier.	事實上，我希望我們早一天抵達。
中：	Why?	為什麼？
外：	I would have liked more time to adjust to the time changes.	我希望有更多的時間調整時差。
中：	When you get to feeling better, I will be happy to show you around the city.	當你覺得好些時，我很樂意帶你到本市四處逛逛。
外：	I will look forward to it.	我會期待的。
中：	Have the secretary page me if you need anything.	如果你有任何需要，叫秘書打給我。
外：	Thank you. I will.	謝謝你。我會。

⊃ 歡迎國外生意伙伴

中： I am glad to see that you got here safely.
我很高興看到你安全抵達這裡。

How is the hotel?
旅館還好吧？

外： Thank you.
謝謝。

The hotel is nice.
旅館很好。

⊃ 與國外客戶寒喧

中： I hope your visit to Taiwan will not have to
be all business.
我希望你來台灣不會全讓商務絆住了。

外： Me, too.
我也希望如此。

I would love to see some of the city.
我想看看這個城市的一些景觀。

🔊 The man who loses his opportunities loses
himself.
（失去機會的人，就是失去了自己。）

⊃ 問候國外商務伙伴

中： Hi.
嗨。

Nice to meet you.
很高興見到你。

How is the office back in America?
在美國的公司還好嗎？

外： Fine.
很好。

I am Mary.
我是瑪麗。

⊃ 表示歡迎國外客戶到來

中： It is nice to finally meet you in person.
很高興終於能見到你本人。

外： You, too!
彼此，彼此。

◀» Character is destiny.
（個性造就了命運。）

注意與人初見面，對方説Nice to meet you.或It's nice to meet you.（很高興見到你！）時，若要用很簡短的英語回應説「我也很高興見到你。」，要説You, too.，而不是Me, too.，因為全句原本應為It's nice to meet you, too.，因為簡化了，只説最後兩字You, too.，與 me too一點關係都沒有。Me, too.的用法在本書其他地方會學到。

Have the secretary page me.的句型，是將have當作「叫別人做事」的意思，英文法上稱為「使役動詞」。這是標準英語用法，英國人較少這樣用，英式英語可能會説Tell the secretary to page me.。使役動詞Have後面的動作，要用原形動詞，如這裡的page（呼叫），假如用Tell時，就不可只用page，要用to page。

每課一句 3秒鐘，強化英語力！

📢 I do not believe we have met yet.
（我相信我們還沒見過面。）

📢 Have we met before?
（我們以前見過面嗎？）

📢 Welcome to the Taipei office.
（歡迎到台北的辦事處來。）

📢 You never know till you tried.
（不試不知。）

🔊 Welcome to Taipei. We are pleased to be doing business with your company.
（歡迎到台北來。我們很高興能和貴公司做生意。）

🔊 Is this your first visit to Taipei?
（這是你第一次訪問台北嗎？）

常用單字 3秒鐘，強化單字力！

flight [flaɪt]		飛行；班機
actually [ˈæktʃʊəlɪ]		實際上
adjust [əˈdʒʌst]		調整
the time changes		時差
safely [ˈseflɪ]		安全的
secretary [ˈsɛkrəˌtɛrɪ]		秘書
in person		本人
welcome [ˈwɛlkəm]		歡迎
visit [ˈvɪzɪt]		拜訪

🔊 Beware of a silent dog and still water.
（小心悶不坑聲的狗和靜止的水。）

47

用英語歡迎朋友

I am on business.
我是來出差的。

精華短句 一學就會！最簡單、迷你的會話

- Is this your first time to Taiwan?
  （這是你第一次到台灣嗎？）

- I was here years ago.
  （很多年前我來過這裡。）

- What brings you here now?
  （這回是什麼風把你吹來？）

- I am on business with my company.
  （我為公司來這裡談生意的。）

- Will you be here long?
  （你會在這裡待很久？）

- My visit is for fun.
  （我是來玩的。）

- I am here on vacation.
  （我來這裡渡假。）

實況會話 靈活運用！會話、聽力同步加強

中：	Nice afternoon, isn't it?	下午天氣真好，不是嗎？
外：	It really is.	的確是。
中：	Is this your first time to Taiwan?	這是你第一次到台灣嗎？
外：	No, I was here years ago.	不，我很多年前來過。
中：	What brings you here this time?	這回是為什麼來這裡呢？
外：	I am on business with my company.	我為公司來這裡做公事的。
中：	Will you be here long?	你會在這裡待很久嗎？
外：	Six months to a year.	六個月到一年。

He who begins many things finishes but few.
（多頭馬車，一事無成。）

⊃ 問外國友人入境動機

中： When did you decide to come to Taiwan?
你什麼時候決定遷來台灣？

外： I didn't.
不是我。

My company transferred me here.
是公司調我來這裡的。

⊃ 詢問來訪原因

中： Is your visit for business, or for fun?
你來是為了生意，還是為了玩？

外： I am here on vacation, so I guess it is for fun.
我是來這裡渡假，所以應該是為了玩。

⊃ 詢問來訪動機

中： Why did you come to Taiwan?
你為什麼來台灣？

外： I volunteered to come and work with a company here.
我自願遷來這裡，在一家公司上班。

秘密都在這裡！

純英語句型解說

I was here years ago.的句型，要注意years前面沒有特定的數字，如3 years ago（三年前）、a few years ago（數年前）等等，只用years ago就是說「好多好多」年以前，究竟幾年都記不得了。

Nice afternoon, isn't it?的句型，在文法上稱為「附加問句」，isn't it的it指天氣而言，全句原是It's a nice afternoon, isn't it?（這個下午真是宜人，不是嗎？）

注意聽MP3，附加問句的語調很重要。最後的尾音，若是向上，表示真的在問對方「是不是」，若是尾音向下，則是普通搭訕，也許是口頭禪，也許是隨口說話帶個「不是嗎？」，表示自己並不武斷，沒有要對方回答的意思。

每課一句 3秒鐘，強化英語力！

🔊 How do you plan to spend your time here in Taiwan?
（你打算怎麼渡過你在台灣的時間？）

🔊 Are you going to stay in Taiwan, or are you here for other reasons?
（你打算長留在台灣，還是為了其他理由來這裡？）

month [mʌnθ]		月
decide [dɪˈsaɪd]		決定
transfer [ˈtrænsfɚ]		調職
for fun		好玩
guess [gɛs]		猜
volunteer [ˌvɑlənˈtɪr]		自願
plan		計劃
spend [spɛnd]		花錢；花時間
reason [ˈrizən]		理由

◄» When you play, play hard. When you work, don't play at all.
（盡情玩樂，努力工作。）

◄» A little learning is a dangerous thing.
（一知半解最危險。）

Unit 9　徵友—電話英語

This is Mary speaking.
我就是瑪麗。

精華短句　一學就會！最簡單、迷你的會話

- Could I speak to Robert please?
  （我可以和羅勃說話嗎？）

- Speaking.
  （我就是。）

- This is she speaking.
  （電話中： 我就是。）

- I was calling about your ad for a friend.
  （我是看到你的徵友廣告，打電話來的。）

- Let's get together for dinner.
  （我們一起去吃晚餐吧！）

- I am going to be living in the country.
  （我會在這個國家住下來。）

- Do you want to meet somewhere for lunch?
  （你要不要在那個地方碰面，吃午餐？）

外：	Hello?	喂？
中：	Could I speak to Robert please?	麻煩一下，我可以和羅勃說話嗎？
外：	This is Robert Speaking.	我就是。
中：	This is Mary. I was calling about your ad in the paper for a friend.	我是瑪麗。我是看到你在報紙上的徵友廣告，打電話來的。
外：	Oh yes. This is my first time in China, and I am wanting to learn the language.	噢，是的。這是我第一次到中國，我想要學好中文。
中：	I am studying English, so I would like someone to practice with, too.	我正在學英語，所以我也想要有人陪我練習。
外：	Let's get together for dinner tonight and meet.	我們今晚一起吃晚餐，碰個面吧！

| 中： | O.K.
That will be fine. | 好。
可以。 |

進階應用 舉一反三！聽說力更上一層樓

⊃ 回覆外國人徵友廣告一

中： I am responding to your ad in the paper.
我是來應徵你在報紙上的廣告。

外： Yes.
是的。

Obviously you speak English.
很顯然你會講英語。

⊃ 回覆外國人徵友廣告二

中： Do you have an ad in the paper for a Chinese friend?
你在報上登徵中國朋友的廣告嗎？

外： I do.
有。

I am going to be living in the country for a couple of years.
我會在這個國家住個幾年。

So, I would like to make some Chinese friends.
所以，我要交一些中國朋友。

⊃ 回覆徵友廣告

中： Hi, this is Robert.
嗨，我叫做羅勃。

I am calling about your ad.
我打電話應徵你的廣告。

外： Great.
好極了。

Do you want to meet somewhere for lunch?
你要找個地方碰面，吃個午餐嗎？

純英語句型解說 秘密都在這裡！

　　隨著通訊的方便，人們日常生活用各種通訊方式，越來越普遍了，不過對學習英語英語的人來說，這可不是個好消息，因為，通訊用語，有其獨特的規則，你沒聽過，有人在用各種通訊方式時，說起話來連音調都會變得怪模怪樣嗎？這是中外皆然，所以各種通訊英語，也有特殊的用法，不會這些用法，各種通訊另外那一頭接聽的人，有時就會完全搞不懂你在說什麼。若要詳細學好通訊方式英語，本公司即將出版各種通訊方式英語書，是最純正的通訊方式英語，值得學習。

在各種通訊方式中表明自己的身份，要用「This is + 人名」的句型。不要用I am ……。

接聽各種通訊，向對方表示自己即是對方要找的人，最簡單的說法是：Speaking.（我就是。），也可以說This is he speaking.（男士）或This is she speaking.（女士），依您的男女性別而定。

每課一句 *3秒鐘，強化英語力！*

📢 Let's meet in person.
（我們親自見個面吧！）

📢 I am a fast learner and a patient teacher.
（我學習的速度很快，而且是個有耐性的老師。）

📢 I am going to be staying in the country for a few years.
（我會在這個國家住幾年。）

📢 Have you had a lot of response to your ad?
（你的廣告有很多回應嗎？）

📢 He is only bright that shines by himself.
（唯有靠自己發光的人，才能真正明亮。）

ad [æd]	廣告
together [tə'gɛðɚ]	一起
respond [rɪ'spɑnd]	回應
obviously ['ɑbvɪəslɪ]	明顯地
a couple of	幾個
somewhere ['sʌm,hwɛr]	某個地方
patient ['peʃənt]	耐心
a lot of	許多

🔊 A little learning is a dangerous thing.
（一知半解，危險之至。）

🔊 A wise man knows his own ignorance; a fool thinks he knows everything.
（智者了解自己的無知，愚者以為自己無所不知。）

🔊 Ask a silly question and you'll get a silly answer.
（問一個愚蠢的問題，你就會得到一個愚蠢的回答。）

🔊 Better to ask the way than go astray.
（多問路不吃虧。）

Unit 10

徵友英文書信

Writing a letter for friends.

寫信交友。

Dear <u>Mary</u>,

    I am writing in response to your ad in the paper for a friend. I have lived in Taiwan all my life, but would like to see <u>America</u> someday. I have been studying <u>English</u> for <u>the past five</u> years. I am excited about having an <u>American</u> to practice with. If you are still looking for someone, my number is: 02-723-8975.

Sincerely yours,

Bill Wang

親愛的瑪麗：

　　我寫信是要應徵你在報紙上登的徵友廣告。我一輩子都住在台灣，但是希望有一天能到美國看看。過去五年我一直在學英文。我很興奮有美國人可以練習英文。如果你還在找人的話，我的電話號碼是02-723-8975。

誠摯的

王比爾

　　英文書信的寫法，有格式，本unit的範文，已是標準英文書信格式，你只要把劃底線的部份換成合適你的字，比如你的大名不會剛好是Bill Wang，把它改一下就行了。

Chapter 2

與老外互助英語

自願當嚮導

I am free this afternoon.
今天下午我有空。

精華短句 一學就會！最簡單、迷你的會話

- Excuse me.
  （對不起。）

- Don't feel like you have to.
  （不用覺得你非這樣做不可。）

- Down the next block.
  （在下個街段。）

- Pleased to meet you.
  （很高興認識你。）

- I would love to show you around the city.
  （我很樂意帶你到本市四處逛逛。）

- That's very kind of you.
  （你實在太好了。）

- That would be great.
  （那太好了。）

- I am feeling really lost.
  （我覺得完全迷失了。）
- Please do not hesitate to ask for help.
  （請不要遲疑，儘管請求幫忙。）

實況會話 靈活運用！會話、聽力同步加強

外：	Excuse me, where is the nearest place to eat?	對不起，最近可以用餐的地方在那裡？
中：	Just down the next block. Where are you from?	就在再過去的下條街段。你是從那裡來的？
外：	I am from Texas.	我從美國德州來。
中：	I am Mary.	我名叫瑪麗。
外：	Pleased to meet you, Mary. I'm Robert.	很高興認識你，瑪麗。我是羅勃。

Chapter 2

與老外互助英語

中：	If you want to, I would love to show you around the city.	如果你願意，我很樂意帶你到本市四處逛逛。
外：	That's very kind of you, but don't feel like you have to.	你太好了，但請不要覺得這是妳的義務。
中：	Oh no. I would like the chance to practice my English.	噢，不會。 我想要有機會練習我的英文。

進階應用 舉一反三！聽說力更上一層樓

⊃ 帶外國朋友觀光城市

中： Would you like some help getting around the city?
你需要幫忙，在城市的四週逛逛嗎？

外： That would be great!
太好了！

⊃ 主動帶外國朋友參觀城市

中： If you need any help getting around the city, just let me know.
如果你需要幫忙在本市四處走走的話，儘管讓我知道。

外： Actually, I wanted to tour the city, but I feel very lost.
事實上，我想遊覽這個都市，但是我不知從何看起。

⊃ 問外國觀客需不需要協助

中： Do you have anyone to help you find your way around?
你有人幫你帶路嗎？

外： No, I don't, but I sure could use some help!
不，沒有，但我確信我需要一些協助！

⊃ 外國觀光客需要導引

外： I am feeling really lost!
我覺得完全迷失了！

中： Well, I would be happy to give you a tour of the city.
我很樂意帶你到本市四處逛逛。

每課一句 3秒鐘，強化英語力！

◀» Do not hesitate. Just ask for help.
（不要猶豫，請求援助。）

◀» I don't mind showing you around.
（我不介意帶你四處遊逛。）

◀))) Call me. Here is my phone number.
（打電話給我。這是我的電話號碼。）

◀))) If you need any help, call me.
（如果你需要任何協助，打電話給我。）

◀))) I am free this afternoon if you want me to show you around the city.
（如果你要我帶你參觀本市，我今天下午有空。）

常用單字 3秒鐘，強化單字力！

nearest ['nɪrəst]	（near的最高級）最靠近
block　 [blɑk]	（市街的）一個街段
would love to	很想要
hesitate ['hɛzə,tet]	猶豫

◀))) Don't claim to know what you don't know.
（不要不懂裝懂。）

◀))) He who asks is a fool for five minutes, but he who does not ask remains a fool forever.
（願意問的人是個五分鐘的傻瓜，不願意問的人是一輩子的傻瓜。）

教朋友學中文

I don't speak Chinese.
我不會講中文。

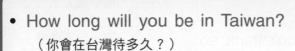

精華短句 一學就會！最簡單、迷你的會話

- How long will you be in Taiwan?
  （你會在台灣待多久？）

- Probably about a year.
  （可能一年左右。）

- I don't think so.
  （我不這樣認為。）

- I don't speak a bit of Chinese.
  （我一句中文都不會說。）

- Have you ever thought about learning Chinese?
  （你有沒有想過學中文？）

- It is not a bad idea.
  （這個主意不錯。）

中：	How long will you be in Taiwan?	你會在台灣待多久？
外：	Probably about a year.	大約一年。
中：	Wow. You will almost be Chinese by the time you go home.	哇。 到你要回家的時候，你幾乎都變成中國人了。
外：	No, I don't think so. I don't speak a bit of Chinese.	不，我不這麼想。 我一點中文都不會說。
中：	I would be glad to teach you the basic language.	我很樂於教你基礎中文。
外：	Really?	真的嗎？
中：	Yes, it would be good practice for me.	是的，對我來說是很好的練習。

🔊 You never know what you can do till you try.
（試了你才知道自己的能耐。）

進階應用 舉一反三！聽說力更上一層樓

⊃ 自願教外國朋友中文

外： I wish I knew what is going on around me.
我真希望知道我的四周到底發生什麼事。

中： If you are willing to learn, I could teach you some Chinese.
如果你願意學習的話，我可以教你一些中文。

⊃ 詢問外國朋友是否想學中文

中： Have you ever thought about learning Chinese?
你有沒有想過要學中文？

外： Actually I have.
事實上，我有。

Why, do you want to teach it?
為何這麼問？你想教中文嗎？

⊃ 外國朋友想要學中文

外： I really have been wanting to learn the language.
我真的一直想學本地語言。

中： If you need a teacher, let me know.
如果你需要老師教，告訴我。

⊃ 自願教外國朋友中文

中： I would be happy to teach you Chinese if you want to learn.
我會樂意教你中文，如果你想學的話。

外： It is not a bad idea.
這個主意倒不錯。

I come to Taiwan a lot.
我經常來台灣的。

每課一句 3秒鐘，強化英語力！

◄》 Would you like some help learning Chinese?
（你學習中文需要幫忙嗎？）

◄》 Are you planning to learn Chinese?
（你打算學中文嗎？）

◄》 If you want to learn the language, let me know.
（如果你想要學本地語言，讓我知道。）

◄》 As we live, so we learn.
（我們活著，所以我們學習。）

常用單字 3秒鐘，強化單字力！

probably [ˈprɑbəblɪ]

　或許

almost [ɔlˈmost]

　幾乎

Chinese　[tʃaɪˈniz]

　中文

by the time

　屆時

teach [titʃ]

　教

basic　[ˈbesɪk]

　基本的

language [ˈlæŋˈwɪdʒ]

　語言

be willing to

　願意

🔊 Knowledge makes humble, ignorance makes proud.
（博學使人謙虛，無知使人驕傲。）

🔊 All men naturally desire to know.
（人的天性皆欲求知。）

找工作

I can help you find a job.
我可以幫你找到工作。

14

精華短句 一學就會！最簡單、迷你的會話

- I just got my permit.
  （我剛拿到工作許可。）

- You have been a big help.
  （你真是我的大貴人。）

- Do you want some help finding a job?
  （你找工作需要幫忙嗎？）

- I may take you up on that.
  （我接受你的好意。）

- I can call and ask to schedule an interview for you.
  （我可以替你打電話，要求安排面談。）

🔊 A man can't do two things at once.
（一心不可二用。）

實況會話 靈活運用！會話、聽力同步加強

中：	Are you going to be staying in Taiwan?	你打算長留在台灣嗎？
外：	Yes, I cannot afford to go back.	是的，我付不起回去的費用。
中：	Are you working?	你工作嗎？
外：	No, I just got my permit two days ago.	不，我二天前才拿到工作許可。
中：	I can help you find a job, but I do not want to impose.	我可以幫你找工作，但是我不想太自作聰明。
外：	No, that would be great. Do you know someone?	不會的，那太棒了。 你有認識的人嗎？
中：	Yes, I will give him your phone number.	是的，我會給他你的電話號碼。
外：	Thanks a lot. You have been a big help.	多謝了。 你一直是我的大貴人。

73

⊃ 自願幫外國朋友找工作

外： I don't know where I am going to get the
money to buy my plane ticket home.
我不知道去哪裡弄買機票回家的錢。

中： If you want a job, I can ask around for you.
如果你想要工作的話，我可以替你四處問問。

⊃ 提供工作點子的說法

中： If you need help finding a job, I can give
you a few ideas.
如果你需要幫助找工作的話，我可以給你一些主意。

外： I may take you up on that.
我接受你的好意。

Thanks.
謝謝。

⊃ 請別人提供意見的說法

中： Do you want some help finding a job?
你需要幫忙找工作嗎？

外： Yes, any ideas you might have would be
great!
是的，你的任何點子對我都很好！

Chapter 2

與老外互助英語

每課一句 3秒鐘，強化英語力！

🔊 I can give your number to a few people.
（我可以把你的電話轉給一些人。）

🔊 I can call and see if there is a job for you.
（我可以替你打電話，看看有沒有工作可以給你。）

🔊 I will be happy to find you a job.
（我樂意替你找工作。）

🔊 Would you like me to set up a job interview for you?
（你要不要我替你安排工作面試？）

🔊 Do you need me to make some calls for you?
（你需要我幫你打幾通電話嗎？）

常用單字 3秒鐘，強化單字力！

afford [ə'fɔrd]	付得起
permit [pɚ'mɪt]	允許
impose [ɪm'poz]	將自己意見強加於人
ask around	四處詢問
schedule ['skɛdʒʊl]	安排時間
interview ['ɪntɚ,vju]	面試
set up	安排

幫忙租房子

Do you want an apartment or a house?

你要公寓，還是房子？

15

精華短句 一學就會！最簡單、迷你的會話

- What you are going to do for housing?
  （你住的問題要怎麼解決？）

- It really will depend on the price.
  （那全要視價格而定。）

- I hear that.
  （我明白了。）

- Give me some advice on where to live.
  （給我一些該住那裡的意見吧。）

- Feel free to call me.
  （儘管打電話給我。）

- Do not think twice about calling me.
  （請不用猶豫打電話給我。）

- You can't have it both ways.
  （事難兩全。）

實況會話 靈活運用！會話、聽力同步加強

外：	I have decided that I am going to stay in Taiwan for the next couple of years.	我已決定下幾年要住在台灣。
中：	Do you know what you are going to do for housing?	你知道住的問題要怎麼解決嗎？
外：	No, I really don't.	不，我真的不知道。
中：	If you need any help picking an area, or any other help, I will be happy to aid you.	如果你需要幫忙選地方，或其他協助，我樂意幫助你。
外：	That is very kind of you.	你真是太好了。
中：	Do you want an apartment or a house?	你要公寓還是房子？
外：	It really will depend on the price.	那全要視價格而定。
中：	I hear that. I will help you look around.	我明白了。 我會幫你四處找找看。

⊃ 願協助定居，怎麼說？

外： I am going to be staying in Taiwan for another year.

我會在台灣多留一年。

中： If you need help getting settled, let me know.

如果你需要幫忙安頓的話，讓我知道。

⊃ 需要別人提供意見，怎麼說？

中： Do you need some help getting settled in permanently?

你需要一些協助，永久定居在這裡嗎？

外： Yes, I would like some advice on where to live.

是的，我需要一些該住哪裡的意見。

⊃ 協助新移民定居下來

中： If I can be of any help as you get established here, let me know.

當你在這裡定居，需要我任何的幫助時，告訴我。

外： I will.

我會的。

I really don't know what I will have to do to get a home.
我真的不知道從何著手找個房子做家。

⊃ 主 伸出協助的手

中： Feel free to call me, if you have any questions while you get your family settled here.
當你在這裡安頓你的家庭，有任何問題時，儘管打電話給我。

外： Thanks.
謝謝。

I don't even know where a hospital is if someone gets hurt!
如果我家裡有人受傷，我甚至還不知道醫院在那裡呢！

每課一句 3秒鐘，強化英語力！

◀》 I am more than happy to help you get settled here.
（我非常樂意幫你在這裡定居下來。）

◀》 Do not think twice about calling me if you need any help.
（如果你需要任何協助，請不要猶豫，打電話給我。）

◀》 Would you like me to keep an eye out for a nice apartment?
（你要不要幫你留意一間好的公寓？）

◀》 Do you need help finding a home?
（你需要協助找個住所嗎？）

常用單字 3秒鐘，強化單字力！

depend [dɪˈpɛnd]	視…而定
stay	停留
settle [ˈsɛtl̩]	定居
permanently [ˈpɝmənəntlɪ]	永久
advice [ədˈvaɪs]	意見
establish [ɛsˈtæblɪʃ]	建立
get hurt	受傷
hospital [ˈhɑspɪtl̩]	醫院
twice [twaɪs]	二次

◀》 Don't worry for tomorrow.
（不要為明天憂慮。）

用英語提出要求

Could you speak slower?
你能不能講慢一點？

- Wait, I am sorry.
  （等一等，對不起。）

- Probably not.
  （也許不會。）

- Not all of it.
  （不是全部。）

- Could you please speak a little slower?
  （能不能請你講慢一點點？）

- I'll slow down.
  （我會放慢速度。）

- I hate to trouble you.
  （我實在不想打擾你。）

- I understand completely.
  （我完全理解。）

- Please, speak a little slower.
  （拜託，說慢一點。）

- Can you understand what I am saying?
  （你能明白我在說什麼嗎？）

- What did you just say?
  （你剛剛說什麼？）

- I am getting lost.
  （我搞糊塗了。）

實況會話 靈活運用！會話、聽力同步加強

外：	(Speak fast) I had the best time last night; we went to the movie and had a big bowl of popcorn, and...	昨晚我度過最好的時光，我們去看電影吃了一大碗爆米花，還有……。
中：	Wait, I am sorry. Could you please speak a little slower?	等一等，對不起。能不能請你說慢一點？

外：	Oh, yes. Was I talking fast?	噢，可以。 我說得太快了嗎？
中：	Probably not, **but I am still learning English.**	也許不算快，但是我才剛在學英文的階段。
外：	I'm sorry. I'll slow down.	對不起。 我會說慢點。
中：	Thank you very much. I hate to trouble you, but I do not want to misunderstand you.	謝謝。 我不想給你惹麻煩，但是我不想誤解你的意思。
外：	I understand completely.	我完全理解。

進階應用 舉一反三！聽說力更上一層樓

⊃ **請人說話慢一點，怎麼說？**

中： Please, speak a little slower.
　　 拜託，請說慢一點。

　　 I am just beginning to learn English.
　　 我才開始學英文。

外： O.K.
好的。

Just remember that when you are teaching me Chinese!
你在教我中文時也要記得講慢一點。

➲ 怕對方聽不明白，怎麼說？

中： Can you understand what I am saying?
你了解我在說什麼嗎？

外： Not all of it.
不是全部了解。

Can you slow down some?
你能不能講慢一點？

➲ 請求放慢說話速度

中： Would you mind talking a little slower?
你介意講慢一點嗎？

外： Not at all.
一點也不。

All you have to do is ask!
你只要提醒我就行了！

◀ A contented man is always rich.
（知足的人最富有。）

84

每課一句 3秒鐘，強化英語力！

◁» I am sorry, what did you just say?
（對不起，你剛剛說什麼？）

◁» I am getting lost, could you talk slower please?
（我弄迷糊了，你能不能說慢一點？）

◁» I am afraid I do not understand, can you
speak slower?
（我恐怕我不明白你的意思，你能不能說慢一點？）

◁» Will you please slow down?
（你能不能說慢一點？）

常用單字 3秒鐘，強化單字力！

slower ['sloɚ]	慢一點（slow的比較級）
went to the movie	看電影（went是go的過去式）
bowl [bol]	碗
popcorn ['pɑpˌkɔrn]	爆米花
fast	快的
misunderstand [mɪsˌʌndɚ'stænd]	誤解
completely [kəm'plitlɪ]	完全地
begin [bɪ'gɪn]	開始
remember [rɪ'mɛmbɚ]	記得

要求教英文

Would you teach me English?
請你教我英文，好嗎？

精華短句 一學就會！最簡單、迷你的會話

- I am self-taught.
  （我是無師自通。）

- Would you mind teaching me English?
  （你介意教我英文嗎？）

- Not at all.
  （一點也不。）

- Of course.
  （當然。）

- I have been trying for some time.
  （我一直在嘗試，有一陣子了。）

- Can you work with me on my English?
  （你能教導我學習英文嗎？）

- I think it would be fun.
  （我想那應該很好玩。）

Chapter 2 與老外互助英語

實況會話 靈活運用！會話、聽力同步加強

外：	Did you go to school to learn English?	你上學校學英文嗎？
中：	No. I am self-taught.	不。 我是無師自通。
外：	I think you speak pretty good.	我認為你說得相當不錯。
中：	I need much more work. Would you mind teaching me English?	我需要更加努力。 你介意教我英文嗎？
外：	Not at all. I did not know that you wanted to learn.	一點也不。 我不知道你想學。
中：	Oh yes. I have been trying for some time.	噢，我想得很呢。 我試著學已經有一陣子了。

◁» All men naturally desire to know.
（人生而有求知欲。－亞里斯多德）

⊃ 要求教英文，怎麼說？

中： Would you be willing to help me learn English?
你願意幫助我學英文嗎？

外： Of course.
當然。

I think it would be fun.
我想那會很好玩。

⊃ 問有沒有在教英文，怎麼說？

中： Do you teach English?
你教英文嗎？

外： Not really, but it would be good practice for me.
不盡然，但是對我而言會是很好的練習。

⊃ 請求教英文的說法

中： Can you work with me on my English?
你可以教導我學英文嗎？

外： Sure, you can come to my house Tuesday nights.
當然，每星期二晚上你可以到我家來。

⊃ **表示仍須努力，怎麼說？**

外： How is your English coming along?
你的英文學得怎樣了？

中： O.K.
還好。

But I think I need some help.
但我想我需要一些協助。

Would you mind teaching me?
你介意教我嗎？

每課一句 3秒鐘，強化英語力！

🔊 Could you teach me English in your spare time?
（你閒暇的時候，可以教我英文嗎？）

🔊 Have you thought about teaching English?
（你有沒有想過教英文？）

🔊 Would it be a problem if I asked you to teach me English?
（如果我要求你教我英文的話，會有困難嗎？）

🔊 Can I come over tonight for an English lesson?
（我今晚可以過來學習英文嗎？）

taught [tɔt]
　教（teach的過去式）

Tuesday ['tuzde]
　星期二

spare [spɛr]
　多餘的

thought [θɔt]
　想（think的過去式）

problem　['prɑbləm]
　問題

come over
　過來

tonight [tə'naɪt]
　今晚

lesson ['lɛsn̩]
　課程

◀)) Live and learn.
　（活到老學到老。）

◀)) Men's natures are all alike; it is their habits
　that carry them far apart.
　（性相近，習相遠。）

付費學英語

I will pay you for English lessons.
我會付你教我英文的錢。

精華短句　一學就會！最簡單、迷你的會話

- Have you thought about teaching English?
  （你有沒有想過教英文？）

- I will think about it.
  （我會考慮看看。）

- That is fine with me.
  （對我來說沒問題。）

- I would not even know how much to charge.
  （我甚至不知道學費該收多少。）

- If I pay you, would you teach me English?
  （如果我付費給你，你願意教我英文嗎？）

- You don't have to pay me.
  （你不必付錢給我。）

- What would you charge for English lessons?
  （上英文課你收費多少錢？）

中：	Have you thought about teaching English when you are off from work?	你有沒有想過下班以後教英文？
外：	I have, but I get very little time at home.	我有，但是我在家的時間很少。
中：	If it makes a difference, I would pay you for your time.	如果你想收費比較好的話，我可以付你鐘點費。
外：	I would not even know how much to charge.	我甚至不知道該收多少學費。
中：	I am sure that you can think of something fair.	我想你一定可以訂出公道價格的。
外：	I will think about it.	我會考慮看看。
中：	Well, if you decide you want the extra money, give me a call.	那麼，如果你決定要賺外快，給我打個電話。

🔊 Custom makes all things easy.
（習慣成自然。）

進階應用 舉一反三！聽說力更上一層樓

⊃ 願意付費上英文課，怎麼說？

中： I will pay you for English Lessons.
我會付你教我英文的錢。

外： That is fine with me.
你要付錢，我沒有問題。。

⊃ 表示不用收費的說法

中： If I pay you, would you mind teaching me English?
如果我付錢給你，你介意教我英文嗎？

外： You don't have to pay me.
你不必付我錢。

We will do the lessons at your house and you can feed me dinner!
我們可以在你家上課，你可以請我吃晚餐！

⊃ 詢問上課收費情形

中： What would you charge for English lessons?
上英文課你要收費多少？

外： How about $10 a lesson?
十美元一堂課如何？

⊃ 交換學對方語言為條件

中： If you like, I can pay you for English lessons.
如果你願意，我可以付你教我英文的費用。

外： Oh no, you don't have to pay me.
噢，不，你不必付我錢。

Maybe you can teach me some Chinese.
或許你可以教我說一些中文。

每課一句 3秒鐘，強化英語力！

🔊 Would you teach English for money?
（你願收費教英文嗎？）

🔊 Do you need some money for the lessons?
（你教課要收一些費用嗎？）

🔊 I will pay for the English lessons if you like.
（如果你願意，我可以付上英文課的錢。）

🔊 What is a fair price for English lessons?
（英文課一般的收費情形如何？）

🔊 It is never too old to learn.
（學習永遠不嫌老。）

常用單字 3秒鐘，強化單字力！

pay
付錢

off from work
下班

difference ['dɪfərəns]
不同

charge [tʃɑrdʒ]
收費

fair [fɛr]
公平

give a call
打電話

extra ['ɛkstrə]
額外

feed (人) dinner
請某人吃晚餐

🔊 You're never too old to learn.
（學習永遠不嫌老。）

🔊 It is never too late to learn.
（學習永遠不嫌晚。）

95

🔊 Learn young, learn fair; learn old, learn more.
（少時學，學得好；老時學，學得多。）

🔊 Knowledge is power.
（知識就是力量。）

🔊 A good book is a light to the soul.
（一本好書是靈魂之光。）

🔊 Knowledge is a treasure but practice is the key to it.
（知識是寶庫，而實踐是鑰匙。）

🔊 Observation is the best teacher.
（觀察是最佳良師。）

🔊 Reading enriches the mind.
（閱讀豐富了心靈。）

🔊 Zeal without knowledge is fire without light.
（熱心而無知，猶如無光之火。）

Chapter 3

興趣與休閒英語

用英語談興趣

I played tennis in high school.
我在高中打過網球。

精華短句　一學就會！最簡單、迷你的會話

- How long have you been playing tennis?
  （你打網球有多久了？）

- I used to play quite a bit myself.
  （我自己以前經常打。）

- Are you free Thursday evenings?
  （每週四晚上，你有沒有空？）

- That sounds great.
  （聽起來很棒。）

- I look forward to seeing you then.
  （我期待到時見到你。）

- I am still becoming familiar with the city.
  （我對這個城市越來越熟悉了。）

- How did you spend your weekend?
  （你怎麼度過你的週末？）

- Do you enjoy camping out?
  （你喜歡露營嗎？）

實況會話 靈活運用！會話、聽力同步加強

中：	Now that you're settled in, what do you do with your free time?	你現在安頓下來了，你有空的時候都做什麼？
外：	I have been working on my tennis game.	我一直在打網球。
中：	**Really**, how long have you been playing?	真的，你打多久了？
外：	I started playing tennis in high school.	我從高中起就打網球。
中：	I used to play quite a bit myself. Since my old tennis partner moved, I haven't played much.	我自己過去也常打。 自從我的老球友搬走之後，我就不常打了。

外：	Are you free Thursday evenings around 6:00? That is the evening I usually play.	每星期四下午六點左右你有空嗎？那是我通常打球的夜晚。
中：	That sounds great.	用星期四晚上打，聽起來很好。
外：	Good, I look forward to seeing you then.	好的，我期待咱們到時再見。

➲ 表示剛開始熟悉環境，怎麼說？

中： What are you doing now that you are settled in?
你既然已安頓好了，你現在都在做什麼？

外： I am still becoming familiar with the city!
我才剛開始在熟悉本市環境！

➲ 問對方休閒做什麼？

中： How did you spend your weekend?
你週末做了什麼事？

外： My sister and I went to the movies.
我和我姐姐去看電影。

⊃ 表示難以置信，怎麼說？

中： Did you see the baseball game last night?
你看昨晚的棒球比賽了嗎？

外： Yes, can you believe that last inning?
看了，那最後一局的情況真難置信！

⊃ 問對方興趣所在，怎麼問？

中： Do you enjoy camping out?
妳喜歡出去露營嗎？

外： Yes, I try to get away every two weeks or so.
是的，我試著每兩星期左右去一次。

每課一句 3秒鐘，強化英語力！

📢 Do you enjoy reading scary books?
（你喜歡看恐怖小說嗎？）

📢 What are you doing on your day off?
（你休假日都做些什麼？）

📢 Do you like rock-and-roll or classical music?
（你喜歡搖滾樂還是古典音樂？）

📢 Do you like movies or television?
（你喜歡看電影還是看電視？）

tennis ['tɛnɪs]	網球
used to	過去常～
partner ['pɑrtnɚ]	夥伴
sound [saʊnd]	聽起來
look forward to	期盼
familiar with	熟悉
weekend ['wik'ɛnd]	週末
believe [bɪ'liv]	相信
inning ['ɪnɪŋ]	一局（棒球）
enjoy [ɪn'dʒɔɪ]	喜歡
camp out	到野外露營
scary ['skɛrɪ]	恐怖的
day off	放假

◀》 Art is long, life is short.
（人生苦短，而學術無涯。）

用英語談喜好

I enjoy camping.
我喜歡露營。

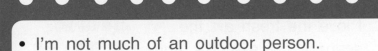

精華短句 一學就會！最簡單、迷你的會話

- I'm not much of an outdoor person.
  （我不是個很喜歡戶外活動的人。）

- What do you like about it?
  （你喜歡它的哪一點？）

- I can't wait.
  （我等不及了。）

- Do you hike or fish on your trips?
  （在旅行時，你會健行或是釣魚嗎？）

- Have fun and be careful.
  （好好玩但小心點哦。）

- My favorite movies are always comedies.
  （我最喜愛的電影總是喜劇。）

- Surfing the Internet is a great way to spend spare time.
  （上網是一個打發空閒時間的好方法。）

中：	I enjoy camping.	我喜歡露營。
外：	Really? I'm not much of an outdoor person. What do you like about it?	真的？我不是個很喜歡戶外活動的人。 你喜歡它哪一點？
中：	I love the fresh air, the scenery, the exercise, and the time to think.	我喜歡新鮮空氣、景緻、運動以及有時間思考。
外：	Do you hike or fish on your trips?	旅遊時，你會健行或是釣魚嗎？
中：	Yes, both. Last trip I fished a little and hiked six miles.	是的，兩者都做。 上次出去，我小釣了一下魚，也健行六英哩。
外：	Did you catch anything?	你釣到什麼魚沒有？

◀» Custom is a second nature.
（習慣是第二天性。）

中：	Yes, but I threw them back. They were too small to keep.	有的，但我把他們放回去了。他們太小，不能留。
外：	When are you going camping again?	你什麼時候要再去露營？
中：	This weekend, I can't wait.	這個週末，我等不及要再去了。
外：	Have fun and be careful.	好好玩但小心點哦。

進階應用 舉一反三！聽說力更上一層樓

⊃ **談論喜好的電影**

中： My favorite movies are always comedies.
我總是喜歡喜劇電影。

外： Really?
真的嗎？

I like suspense myself.
我自己是喜歡懸疑 的電影。

⊃ 談網際網路

中： Surfing the Internet is a great way to spend spare time.

上網是打發空閒時間的一個好方法。

外： I'm still not on-line.

我還沒有連線。

⊃ 談自己的喜好

中： I enjoy documentaries on TV.

我喜歡電視上的記錄片。

外： They are O.K.

記錄片是還好啦。

But I like comedies.

但我喜歡喜劇。

⊃ 談休閒喜好

中： In my spare time, I like to paint.

閒暇時我喜歡畫畫。

外： I would love to see your work.

我想看看你的作品。

I collect artwork.

我有在收藏藝術品。

每課一句 3秒鐘，強化英語力！

🔊 I love to fish on the weekends.
（每週末，我喜歡去釣魚。）

🔊 My favorite book is "Interview with a Vampire".
（我最喜歡的書是「夜訪吸血鬼」。）

🔊 I enjoy reading in my spare time.
（閒暇時，我喜歡閱讀。）

🔊 Cooking is a hobby of mine.
（烹飪是我的嗜好之一。）

常用單字 3秒鐘，強化單字力！

hobby ['hɑbɪ]	嗜好
outdoor ['aʊt'dor]	戶外的
fresh	新鮮的
scenery ['sinərɪ]	風景
exercise ['ɛksəˌsaɪz]	運
hike	健行
catch	抓
threw [θru]	丟、投（throw的過去式）

Chapter 3

興趣與休閒英語

107

careful ['kɛrfəl]	小心的
favorite ['fævərɪt]	最喜歡的
comedy ['kɑmədɪ]	喜劇
suspense [səs'pɛns]	懸疑劇
surf [sɝf]	衝浪；漂游
Internet	國際網際網路
documentary [ˌdɑkjə'mɛntərɪ]	文件、記錄片
paint	畫畫
collect [kə'lɛkt]	收藏
artwork	藝術品
vampire ['væmpaɪr]	吸血鬼

◀» Future gains are uncertain.
（活在當下。／別指望尚未實現的收益。）

◀» Read much, but not too many books.
（多讀書，但不要讀很多書。）

用英語談運動

Did you see the basketball game?
你看那場籃球賽沒有？

精華短句 一學就會！最簡單、迷你的會話

- I was on the edge of my seat.
  （我緊張得都快坐不住了。）

- There is nothing like being in the action.
  （沒有什麼可以比得上臨場感。）

- Do you want to play golf on Friday?
  （你星期五要不要打高爾夫球？）

- The game is out of town.
  （比賽是在外地舉行。）

- That was quite a move.
  （那個動作美極了！）

- How is six o'clock in the morning?
  （早上六點如何？）

- Are the fish biting?
  （魚吃不吃餌？）

中：	Did you see the basketball game last night?	你看昨晚的籃球賽沒有？
外：	Yes, can you believe it went into three overtimes?	有啊，你相信比賽竟然延長了三次？
中：	I know I was on the edge of my seat.	我知道自己緊張得都快坐不住了。
外：	I wish I could go to the next game, but it is out of town.	我希望我能去看下場比賽，但它在外地打。
中：	Me, too. There is nothing like being in the action.	我也一樣。 沒有什麼可以比得上臨場感。
外：	You have to admit the best part of the game was the slam dunk from the free throw line.	你得承認這場比賽最精彩的部份，是從罰球線灌籃那一球。
中：	You're right. That was quite a move.	你說的對。 那個動作真是美極了。

進階應用 舉一反三！聽說力更上一層樓

⊃ 邀人打高爾夫，怎麼說？

中： Do you want to play golf on Friday?
妳星期五要不要打高爾球？

外： That sounds good.
那聽起來很不錯。

How is six o'clock in the morning?
早上六點如何？

⊃ 釣魚時閒聊

中： Are the fish biting?
魚吃不吃餌？

外： Not yet.
還沒來吃呢。

⊃ 婉拒邀請的說法

中： Are you going to the tennis match on Sunday?
星期日，你要不要去看網球賽？

外： No, I have a wedding to go to.
不能去，我要參加一個婚禮。

中： Are you going to run tomorrow if it rains?
如果明天下雨，你會去跑步嗎？

外： No, I will probably go to the gym instead.
不，我可能會去體育館吧。

每課一句 3秒鐘，強化英語力！

🔊 Are you free Saturday for tennis?
（星期六你有空打網球嗎？）

🔊 Do you walk or ride when you play golf?
（當你打高爾夫時，你是走路還是開車？）

🔊 Where is the closest jogging trail?
（最靠近這裡的慢跑跑道在哪？）

🔊 What gym do you work out at?
（你在那一個健身房健身？）

🔊 Who made it to the play-offs in basketball?
（籃球是哪隊打入複賽？）

🔊 Books and friends should be few but good.
（朋友與書，貴精不在多。）

常用單字 3秒鐘，強化單字力！

basketball ['bæskɪt,bɔl]	籃球	
overtime ['ovɚ,taɪm]	延長比賽	
edge ['ɛdʒ]	邊緣	
match [mætʃ]	比賽	
wedding ['wɛdɪŋ]	婚禮	
gym [dʒɪm]	體育館；健身房	
instead [ɪn'stɛd]	相反地	
work out	健身	
jogging trail	慢跑道	
play-off	季後賽；複賽	

🔊 There is no royal road to learning.
（學問無捷徑。）

用英語談音樂

Who sings that song?
那首歌是誰唱的？

精華短句 一學就會！最簡單、迷你的會話

- That's what I thought.
  （我也是這麼想。）

- I like classical better.
  （我比較喜歡古典音樂。）

- What is your favorite music?
  （你最喜歡的音樂是那一類？）

- Piano is my favorite type of classical music.
  （鋼琴是我最喜歡的古典音樂類型。）

- Rock and roll is my favorite.
  （搖滾樂是我的最愛。）

- I wish I could play the guitar.
  （我希望我會彈吉他。）

- Turn down your radio please.
  （請把收音機關小聲。）

實況會話 靈活運用！會話、聽力同步加強

中：	Who sings that song?	那首歌是誰唱的？
外：	I think it's the Rolling Stones.	我想是滾石樂團。
中：	That's what I thought. They are my favorite group.	我也是這麼想。他們是我最喜歡的樂團。
外：	Really? I like classical better.	真的？我比較喜歡古典音樂。
中：	Do you enjoy piano or orchestra music more?	你喜歡鋼琴，還是比較喜歡弦樂？
外：	Piano is my favorite type of classical music.	鋼琴是我最喜歡的古典音樂類型。
中：	I like some piano music, but rock and roll is my favorite.	我喜歡某些鋼琴音樂，但是搖滾樂是我的最愛。

Chapter 3

興趣與休閒英語

⊃ 詢問喜歡的電台

中： What is your favorite radio station?
你最喜歡的廣播電台是那一個？

外： I listen to the top forty station.
我聽「排行榜40」電台。

⊃ 詢問有沒有參加音樂會

中： Have you been to any good concerts lately?
你最近有沒有去聽什麼好的音樂會？

外： No, I haven't had time.
不，我沒有時間。

⊃ 但願自己會彈樂器，怎麼說？

中： I wish I could play the guitar.
我希望我會彈吉他。

外： You should think about taking lessons.
你應該考慮去上課。

◀» The more noble, the more humble.
（人愈高尚，愈謙虛。）

⤹ 要求把收音機關小聲

中： Turn down your radio please. I can't hear a thing.

請把你的收音機關小聲一點，我什麼都聽不見。

外： Sorry.

對不起。

That's my favorite song.

那是我最喜歡的歌。

每課一句 3秒鐘，強化英語力！

◀》 Do you prefer classical to soft jazz?
（你喜歡古典音樂勝於輕爵士樂嗎？）

◀》 Where is a good place to hear live music?
（那裡是聽現場音樂的好地方？）

◀》 I have been playing the piano for five years.
（我彈鋼琴有五年的時間了。）

◀》 When do you offer lessons for the piano?
（你什麼時候教鋼琴課程？）

◀》 What radio station do you listen to?
（你都聽那一個電台？）

◀》 When sorrow is asleep, wake it not.
（傷心舊事別重提。）

117

3秒鐘，強化單字力！

piano [pɪˈæno]	鋼琴
orchestra [ˈɔrkɪstrə]	管弦樂
concert [ˈkɑnsɚt]	音樂會
lately [ˈletlɪ]	最近
prefer A to B	喜歡A勝於B
soft jazz	輕爵士樂
offer [ˈɔfɚ]	提供
radio station	廣播電台
listen [ˈlɪsn̩]	聽

📣 It is easy to be wise after the event.
（經一事長一智。）

📣 He who begins many things finishes but few.
（多頭馬車，一事無成。）

用英語談跳舞

We had a small party.
我們辦了一個小型舞會。

精華短句 一學就會！最簡單、迷你的會話

- Where is the party at?
  （舞會在那裡舉行？）

- What time does it start?
  （那是幾點開始？）

- Thanks for all the help.
  （謝謝你所有的協助。）

- No problem.
  （沒問題。）

- Where is a good place to dance?
  （那裡是跳舞的好地方？）

- We want to give you a going away party.
  （我們想要替你舉行一場告別舞會。）

中：	Are you going to John's birthday party this weekend?	這個週末你要參加約翰的生日舞會嗎？
外：	Yes. Do you know if it is casual or semi-formal party?	要。你知道舞會要穿半正式還是休閒衣服？
中：	It is casual.	穿普通衣服就可以。
外：	Where is the party at?	舞會在那裡舉行？
中：	John's house.	在約翰的家。
外：	What time does it start?	舞會什麼時候開始？
中：	Around 6:30 P.M.	大約晚上六點半。
外：	Thanks for all the help.	謝謝你所有的協助。
中：	No problem. I will see you there.	別客氣，咱們到那裡再見吧。

進階應用 舉一反三！聽說力更上一層樓

⊃ 詢問那裏有好的舞廳

中： Where is a good place to dance?
那裏是跳舞的好地方？

外： The nightclub up the street plays good music.
街上的午夜俱樂部音樂奏得不錯。

⊃ 公司辦舞會

中： Are you coming to the company party?
公司的舞會你會來參加嗎？

外： Yes, I am coming.
會，我會來。

⊃ 為同事舉行送別舞會

中： Before you move, we want to give you a going away party.
在你搬遷之前，我們想要替你辦一場送別舞會。

外： Thanks, everyone.
謝謝大家。

My last day is in two weeks.
我上班最後一天是兩星期後。

中：I heard the party was kind of dull.
我聽說那個舞會有些無聊。

外：It was O.K.
還好啦。

We only had a small party.
我們只不過辦了一個小舞會而已。

每課一句 3秒鐘，強化英語力！

◀》 What is the dress code for the party?
（舞會規定穿什麼衣服？）

◀》 When does the party for Susan start?
（替蘇珊舉辦的舞會什麼時候開始？）

◀》 Did you all have fun last night?
（昨晚你們玩得愉快嗎？）

◀》 Where is a good local club?
（本地那裡有好的俱樂部？）

◀》 Are you coming to the party tomorrow night?
（你明晚要不要來參加舞會？）

◀》 Necessity is the mother of invention.
（需要為發明之母。）

常用單字 3秒鐘，強化單字力！

birthday [′bɝθ,de]
　生日

party [′pɑrtɪ]
　舞會

casual　[′kæʒʊəl]
　普通衣服

semi-formal
　半正式的

dance
　跳舞

nightclub
　午夜俱樂部

dull [dʌl]
　無趣的

local　[′lokḷ]
　當地

Thought is the seed of action.
（思想為行動之種子。）

Experience keeps a dear school.
（經驗是最佳教育。）

Experience must be bought.
（必須付出代價學到經驗。）

It is never too late to mend.
（亡羊補牢猶未晚也。）

It is never too late to apologize.
（道歉不嫌晚。）

Let bygones be bygones.
（既往不咎。）

Kind words soften anger.
（好聽的話使怒氣緩和。）

Chapter 4

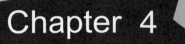

生活英語

購物

The prices are good.
價格很便宜。

精華短句　一學就會！最簡單、迷你的會話

- I am out of food and milk.
  （我沒有食物和牛奶了。）

- I have to run to the grocery store.
  （我必須到雜貨店買東西。）

- They are a little expensive.
  （他們的東西貴了一點。）

- What store do you shop at?
  （你都在哪家商店購物？）

- Thanks for the advice.
  （謝謝你提供意見。）

- You should try my store.
  （到我購物的店試試看。）

- My favorite way to shop is through mail.
  （郵局是我最喜歡的購物方式。）

- I get all the catalogs.
  （我收到一大堆購物型錄。）

實況會話 靈活運用！會話、聽力同步加強

中：	What are you doing tonight?	你今天晚上要做什麼？
外：	I have to run to the grocery store.	我必須到雜貨店買東西。
中：	Don't you hate fighting the crowds on the weekends?	週末去人擠人，難道你不討厭嗎？
外：	Yes, but I am out of food and milk.	我是討厭，但我已經沒有食品和牛奶了。
中：	What store do you shop at?	你都在哪家商店買東西？
外：	The small one just down the street. I like their generic brand.	就在街上過去的那家小店。 他們賣的仿名牌貨品，我還喜歡。

◀» Is this item on sale?
（這個商品正在拍賣嗎？）

◀» If you don't have this bike in stock, can I
have the floor model?
（如果這腳踏車沒有存貨，我可不可以要那部展示的樣品？）

◀» Do you take credit cards?
（你們收信用卡嗎？）

◀» Can I return this item if it is not what I
need?
（如果這個貨不符我所需，我能退還嗎？）

◀» When does the sale end?
（拍賣到什麼時候截止？）

grocery store	食品雜貨店
shop	（動詞）採購
fight [faɪt]	相爭
crowds [kraʊdz]	人潮
generic [dʒəˈnɛrɪk]	一般的
brand	品牌

generic brand	（仿名牌的）類似品牌
expensive [ɪkˈspɛnsɪv]	昂貴的
order [ˈɔrdɚ]	訂購
magazine [ˌmægəˈzin]	雜誌
catalog [ˈkætəlɔg]	型錄
on sale	拍賣
stock [stɑk]	存貨
credit card	信用卡

🔊 A fault confessed is half redressed.
（肯認錯是改過的一半。）

⊃ 送全部人一樣的東西，怎麼說？

外： What are getting your family for a souvenir?
你要替你家人買什麼當紀念品？

中： They are all getting post cards.
我給他們全都買明信片。

⊃ 要求友人買紀念品

中： This baseball cap is a souvenir from my trip to America.
這頂棒球帽是我到美國旅行時的紀念品。

外： Really? You will have to get me one if you go back.
真的，如果你再去美國的話，你可得幫我買一頂。

⊃ 詢問在那裡買到紀念品

外： Where did you get those earrings?
你在哪裡買到這些耳環？

中： My friend got them for me in America.
我的朋友在美國替我買的。

◀》 When you play, play hard. When you work, don't play at all.
（盡情玩樂，努力工作。）

つ 想知道是否有折扣

外： Do you get a discount if you buy several T-shirts?
如果你買好幾件Ｔ恤，有折扣嗎？

中： I don't know. Let's ask the salesperson.
我不知道。我們問問售貨員吧。

每課一句 3秒鐘，強化英語力！

◀ッ How much are shirts and sweat shirts?
（襯衫和長袖T恤要多少錢？）

◀ッ Do you take credit cards?
（你收信用卡嗎？）

◀ッ My favorite souvenir is my key chain from America.
（我最喜歡的紀念品是在美國買的鑰匙鍊。）

◀ッ When I go on vacation, do you want me to bring you a souvenir?
（當我去渡假的時候，你要不要我幫你帶紀念品？）

◀ッ What would you like if you were buying a souvenir?
（如果你買紀念品，你要買什麼？）

Chapter 4

生活英語

中：	Have you been to the inventory sale at the department store?	你去看過百貨公司的清倉拍賣了嗎？
外：	No, what do they have?	沒有，他們有什麼在拍賣呢？
中：	All shorts, shirts and other summer attire is half off.	短褲，襯衫和其他夏天服裝，一律半價。
外：	Wow, what a deal!	哇，那多划算哪！
中：	I know. I bought three pairs of shorts and four shirts.	我知道。 我買了三件短褲和四件襯衫。
外：	Do you know when the sale ends?	你知道拍賣什麼時候結束？
中：	It ends tomorrow.	明天結束。
外：	Well, I need to get going then.	那我得快去。
中：	Have fun. See you tomorrow.	好好玩吧，明天見。

進階應用 舉一反三！聽說力更上一層樓

⊃ 詢問友人在何處購得商品

中： What store do you buy your shoes from?
你的鞋子是在那個商店買的？

外： I buy my shoes from a discount shoe store.
我在大型折扣鞋店買的。

⊃ 詢問營業時間，怎麼說？

外： What time does the mall open?
大型購物商店什麼時候開始營業？

中： I think it opens at 9:00 am.
我想是早上九點開門。

⊃ 談論百貨公司的拍賣

外： Did you hear about the big sale at the department store?
你知道有家百貨公司在大拍賣嗎？

中： Yes, I went yesterday.
是的，我昨天去過了。

⊃ 到商店換貨，怎麼說？

外： Can I exchange my gift for another item?
我可以把收到的贈品換其他商品嗎？

兌換錢幣

Can you break a large bill?
你能把大鈔找開嗎？

精華短句　一學就會！最簡單、迷你的會話

- Does the store accept checks?
  （商店收支票嗎？）

- Cash only.
  （只收現金。）

- Can you break a $100 bill?
  （一百元美金大鈔你能找得開嗎？）

- Let me ring up your order.
  （讓我先把你的貨價打入收銀機。）

- Can you cash traveler's checks?
  （你能兌現旅行支票嗎？）

- Can I write a personal check?
  （我可以開個人支票嗎？）

- I need to witness the signature.
  （我得親眼看見你簽名。）

實況會話 靈活運用！會話、聽力同步加強

顧客：	Hello, how are you?	哈囉，你好嗎？
店員：	Fine, thank you. Are these your items?	我很好，謝謝。 這些是你要的商品嗎？
顧客：	Yes. Does the store accept checks?	是的，你們商店收支票嗎？
店員：	No, cash only.	不，只收現金。
顧客：	Can you break a large bill?	你能夠把大鈔找開嗎？
店員：	Yes, let me ring up your order.	可以，讓我先把你的貨價打入收銀機。

進階應用 舉一反三！聽說力更上一層樓

➲ 詢問是否可以換零錢

中： Can you make change for the coke machine?
你能夠換可樂販賣機的零錢給我嗎？

上銀行

I need a bank account.
我要開一個銀行戶頭。

精華短句　一學就會！最簡單、迷你的會話

- **That would be great.**
  （那太好了。）

- **I can go with you.**
  （我可以和你一起去。）

- **I have a hard time communicating.**
  （我說話溝通有問題。）

- **Can I get duplicate checks?**
  （我可以訂購有存根的支票嗎？）

- **If I lose my checks, what do I do?**
  （萬一我遺失支票，該怎麼辦？）

- **What are the bank hours?**
  （銀行營業時間是幾點？）

實況會話 靈活運用！會話、聽力同步加強

外：	I need a bank account.	我需要開一個銀行戶頭。
中：	I use the bank just down the road.	我的銀行就在這條路不遠的地方。
外：	Can I get an account there without being a citizen?	我不是本國人，可以在那裡開戶嗎？
中：	Oh, yes. I can go with you if you want.	噢，可以。 你願意的話，我可以與你一起去。
外：	That would be great. I am still having a hard time communicating.	那太好了。 我說話溝通還有問題。
中：	No problem. We can go at lunch.	沒關係。 我們午餐時間去吧。
外：	Thanks a lot!	多謝了。

Chapter 4

生活英語

觀光

I can arrange a tour for you.
我可以為你安排觀光。

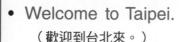

精華短句 一學就會！最簡單、迷你的會話

- Welcome to Taipei.
  （歡迎到台北來。）

- That sounds great.
  （那太好了。）

- Leave a message for me.
  （留話給我。）

- Enjoy your stay.
  （祝你在本地愉快！）

- What are the best spots to see?
  （最好的觀光景點是哪裡？）

- Are there guided tours for tourist?
  （有沒有專給旅客辦的有導遊的觀光團？）

- Let me show you the sights.
  （讓我帶你參觀。）

實況會話 靈活運用！會話、聽力同步加強

中：	Welcome to Taiwan.	歡迎到台灣來。
外：	Thank you. I just arrived last night.	謝謝你，我昨晚才抵達。
中：	You will have to see the sights.	你一定要好好觀光才行。
外：	I would love to, but I'm not familiar with this city.	我當然想觀光，但我對此都市不熟。
中：	I can arrange a tour for you if you are interested.	妳若有興趣，我可以幫妳安排一趟旅遊。
外：	That sounds great. Leave a message for me at the hotel.	聽起來，很有意思。請你打電話到飯店留話給我。
中：	I will arrange that today. Enjoy your stay.	我今天會安排。祝你在本地愉快！

Chapter 4

生活英語

151

Unit
29

I'd like to have a two-bedroom
apartment.

- That may not be available.
- What are the major obligations to rent?
- The sooner the better.
- If you need any help, let me know.
- I have to get an apartment soon.
- Do you know if there are any vacant

租房子

I'd like to have a two-bedroom apartment.
我要租一間兩房公寓。

精華短句　一學就會！最簡單、迷你的會話

- That may not be available.
  （那可能得不到。）

- What are the major obligations to rent?
  （租房子有什麼義務？）

- The sooner the better.
  （愈快愈好。）

- If you need any help, let me know.
  （你若需要協助，通知我。）

- I have to get an apartment soon.
  （我必須快點找個公寓。）

- Do you know if there are any vacant apartments?
  （你知道有沒有空的公寓？）

實況會話 靈活運用！會話、聽力同步加強

外：	I just moved here from America. I need to rent an apartment.	我剛從美國搬來。 我需要租一間公寓。
中：	I can take you out and show you some of the buildings in the area.	我可以帶你出去，把附近的房子展示給你看。
外：	I would like a two bedroom, two bath apartment.	我想要兩房雙衛的公寓。
中：	That may not be available, but we can look.	那也許沒有，不過我們可以找找看。
外：	Sounds good. When do you want to go?	那好。 妳幾時要去看？
中：	We can go at lunch and get food on the way.	我們可以中午去看，順便在途中買東西吃。

🔊 Don't claim to know what you don't know.
（不要不懂裝懂。）

🔊 Do you need any help finding a nice place?
（你需要協助找個理想的地方嗎？）

🔊 Have you been able to locate a good apartment?
（你能找到好公寓嗎？）

🔊 I can show you some of the buildings near here.
（我可以帶你看附近的好房子。）

常用單字 3秒鐘，強化單字力！

apartment [ə'pɑrtmənt]	公寓
major ['medʒɚ]	主要的
available [ə'veləbḷ]	可得的
obligation [ˌɑblə'geʃən]	義務
at least	最少
pet [pɛt]	寵物
allow [ə'laʊ]	允許
vacant ['vekənt]	空的
locate [lo'ket]	找到

介紹本地美食

Let me take you to lunch.
讓我帶你去吃午餐。

精華短句 一學就會！最簡單、迷你的會話

- Let me show you the best dishes.
  （讓我介紹最好的美食給你。）

- Do you want to try the local foods?
  （你要不要試試本地食物？）

- I will show you some of the best dishes.
  （我會介紹你一些最好的食物。）

- I have been wondering what to try.
  （我一直在想，該試吃什麼東西？）

- That sounds wonderful.
  （那太好了。）

- Why don't we go to lunch this afternoon?
  （今天下午我們何不一道去吃午餐？）

實況會話 靈活運用！會話、聽力同步加強

中：	How long have you been here now?	你到這裡多久了？
外：	Almost two weeks.	差不多兩星期了。
中：	Have you had much local food?	你吃過很多本地食物了嗎？
外：	Not really. I have not known where to go!	沒有。我根本還不知道去哪裡吃！
中：	Let me take you to lunch. I will show you some of the best dishes.	讓我帶你去吃午餐。我會介紹你一些最好的食物。
外：	That sounds wonderful.	那太妙了。
中：	I will meet you at your desk in an hour.	一小時後我來你辦公處碰頭。

📣 Reading enriches the mind.
（閱讀豐富了心靈。）

160

進階應用 舉一反三！聽說力更上一層樓

⊃ 提議介紹美食的說法

M: Do you want to try some of the local foods?
妳要不要試試本地食物？

W: Yes.
要。

I have been wondering what to try!
我一直在想，要試吃什麼東西呢？

⊃ 提議去吃當地食物的說法

M: Why don't we go to lunch this afternoon so you can try some of the local food?
我們今天下午何不去吃午餐？那你也可以試試本地食物。

W: That sounds great.
那太好了。

Let me know when you want to go.
你幾時要去就告訴我。

⊃ 建議朋友吃當地美食的說法

M: You have to try the local food before you leave.
在你離開前，你得試試本地美食才行。

W: Where should I go?
（我要到哪裡去吃？）

📢 I can show you the best places to eat local food.
（我可以帶你去最好的地方吃本地食物。）

📢 Are you interested in trying local food?
（你有興趣試試本地食物嗎？）

📢 If you want to try local food, I will be happy to go with you and tell you what is what.
（你若有興趣試試本地食物，我樂意帶你去，並告訴你哪些是哪些東西。）

📢 You cannot leave before you try the local foods; they are too good!
（你沒試過本地食物之前不能離開；它們太好吃了。）

dish	菜色
wonderful ['wʌndəfəl]	太好了
local ['lokl̩]	本地的
wonder ['wʌndər]	猜想

Unit 31

上餐廳

Where do you want to eat dinner?

你要上哪裡吃晚餐？

精華短句 一學就會！最簡單、迷你的會話

- Do you have plans for dinner?
  （你有沒有約人一起吃晚餐？）

- Would you like to join me?
  （要不要跟我一道去？）

- Do you think reservations are needed?
  （你想須要先訂座嗎？）

- It is on a first-come-first-serve basis.
  （他們是先到先得。）

- The restaurant next door is great.
  （隔壁那家餐館很好。）

- How are the restaurant prices here?
  （此地餐館收費如何？）

- They are fair.
  （它們還算公道。）

中：	Do you have plans for dinner?	有沒有約人吃晚餐？
外：	No, why do you ask?	沒有，為何有此一問？
中：	There is a new restaurant downtown I would like to try. Would you like to join me?	市中心有家新餐館，我想試試。要不要跟我一道去？
外：	That sounds nice. What time do you want to go?	主意不錯。你幾點要去？
中：	How about 7:00 P.M?	下午七點如何？
外：	Do you think reservations are needed?	你想須要先訂座嗎？
中：	My coworker said it is on a first-come-first-serve basis.	我同事說那家餐廳是先到先坐。
外：	Then I will meet you there at 7:00 P.M.	那我就七點與你在那家餐廳碰面。

進階應用 舉一反三！聽說力更上一層樓

⊃ 推薦餐廳，怎麼說？

M: The restaurant next door is great.
隔壁那家餐館很好。

W: I have never eaten there.
我從沒在那裡吃過飯。

⊃ 邀請朋友上館子的說法

M: Do you want to go to the restaurant for lunch?
你想不想上館子吃午餐？

W: Yes.
好啊。

I am very hungry.
我好餓噢。

⊃ 有關餐館收費的說法

W: How are the restaurant prices here?
此地餐館收費如何？

M: I think they are fair.
我想還算合理。

You can have a nice lunch for about $6.
大約六美元就可讓你好好享用一頓午餐。

🔊 I'll show you the new restaurant downtown.
（我帶你去市中心的新飯店。）

🔊 Have you eaten yet?
（你吃過飯了嗎？）

🔊 Do you want to have lunch with me at the restaurant down the street?
（你要不要和我到街那頭的餐館吃午飯？）

🔊 Where do you want to eat dinner?
（你想上哪裡吃晚餐？）

常用單字 3秒鐘，強化單字力！

restaurant [ˈrɛstərənt]		餐館；飯店
join [dʒɔɪn]		加入
reservation [ˌrɛzəˈveʃən]		訂座
coworker [ˌkoˈwɝkɚ]		同事
serve [sɝv]		服務
first-come-first-serve		先到先得
hungry [ˈhʌŋgrɪ]		餓

Unit 32

付帳

How much is the check?
帳單是多少？

精華短句 一學就會！最簡單、迷你的會話

- The total of the check is NT$2,400.
  （帳單一共是新台幣兩千四百元。）

- Let's at least split the check.
  （讓我們平分付帳吧。）

- I want to pay cash.
  （我要付現金。）

- Do we pay here or at the front?
  （我們是在此付錢還是到前面去付？）

- We are in a hurry.
  （我們在趕時間。）

🔊 Future gains are uncertain.
（活在當下。）

中：	That was a good meal. How much is the check?	這餐飯吃得過癮。帳單多少？
外：	The total is $24.	一共二十四美元。
中：	I'll get dinner.	我來付錢。
外：	No. Please let me pay.	不。請讓我付吧。
中：	No. I planned on buying you dinner.	不。我計畫好要請你吃飯的。
外：	That is kind of you. Let's at least split the check.	你太客氣了。讓我們各付一半吧。
中：	No. You leave the tip and I will pay the bill.	不。你留小費，我付帳單好了。
外：	Thanks!	那就謝了。

進階應用 舉一反三！聽說力更上一層樓

⊃ 要求侍者將帳單平分，怎麼說？

客人： Can you split the check four ways for my friends and I?
可否請妳將帳單平分成四份給我和我的友人？

侍者： Yes, I will be right back.
好，我馬上回來。

⊃ 問侍者不同付帳法，怎麼說？

客人： I want to pay cash and she wants to pay with credit.
我要付現金，她要用信用卡。

Can we?
我們可以這樣付錢嗎？

客人： Yes.
可以的。

I will be back in a minute with the separate checks.
我馬上把帳單分開再回來。

⊃ 問在哪裡付錢？

客人： Do we pay here or at the front?
我們是在此付錢還是到前面付？

客人：　You pay here.
在這裡付。

➲ 要侍者快收帳找錢，怎麼說？

客人：　We are in a hurry.
我們在趕時間。

Can we get change for our bill?
可否找錢給我們？

客人：　Yes, I will be right back.
好的，我馬上回來。

每課一句 3秒鐘，強化英語力！

◀》 Do you accept checks?
（你們收支票嗎？）

◀》 Is gratuity added in?
（服務費已經加在帳單上了嗎？）

◀》 I need some small bills with my change.
（找零錢時，請給我小鈔。）

◀》 Where do we pay?
（我們在哪付錢？）

◀》 Heaven helps those who help themselves.
（天助自助者。）

常用單字 3秒鐘，強化單字力！

tip

小費

split [splɪt]
平分

separate ['sɛpəˌret]
分開

front [frʌnt]
前面

hurry [hɝɪ]
急

gratuity [grə'tjuətɪ]
服務費

add [æd]
加

🔊 Pride goes before a fall.
（驕兵必敗。）

171

請喝酒

What can I bring you to drink?
你要喝什麼？

精華短句 一學就會！最簡單、迷你的會話

- I like to pay as-you-go.
  （我喝酒喜歡酒一來就付現金。）

- You need a credit card
  （你需要一張信用卡。）

- Can we transfer our tab to the dinner table?
  （我們可以把這裡的帳轉到用餐的帳上嗎？）

- Let me buy you a drink.
  （讓我請妳喝酒。）

- Can I order a drink here and transfer it to my dinner tab?
  （我可以在這裡訂酒，把帳一起轉到用餐的帳單上嗎？）

🔊 There is no royal road to learning.
（學問無捷徑。）

實況會話 靈活運用！會話、聽力同步加強

侍：	Good evening. What can I bring you to drink?	晚安。你們想喝點什麼？
中：	I would like a glass of wine and my friend wants a champagne.	我要一杯葡萄酒，我朋友要香檳。
侍：	Would you like to start a tab or pay as-you-go?	你們要先記在點酒單上還是要付現？
中：	Start a tab, please.	記在點酒單上。
侍：	I need a credit card.	我需要一張信用卡。
中：	O.K. Do you accept Master card?	好。你們收Master卡嗎？
侍：	Yes, we do. I will start you a tab and be right back with your drinks.	是，我們收。我會寫「點酒單」，馬上就把你們的酒送來。

中：	Can we transfer our tab to the dinner table?	我們可以把點酒帳單轉到用餐的帳嗎？
侍：	Yes, let me know when your ready to move.	可以，當你們要移到用餐部時，告訴我。

進階應用 舉一反三！聽說力更上一層樓

⊃ 要請朋友喝酒，怎麼說？

中： Let me buy you a drink.
讓我請妳喝酒。

外： Are you sure? Thanks!
真的嗎？謝謝了。

⊃ 問收不收支票？

中： Do you accept checks at the bar?
你們酒吧台收支票嗎？

侍： No, only cash or credit cards.
不，只收現金或信用卡。

◀》 Books and friends should be few but good.
（朋友與書，貴精不在多。）

⊃ 酒錢和飯錢一起付，怎麼說？

中： Can I order a drink here and transfer it to my dinner tab?
我可以在這裡訂酒，把帳一起轉到用餐的帳單上嗎？

侍： Yes, that will not be a problem.
可以，那沒有問題。

⊃ 拒絕喝酒的說法

外： Would you like to have a drink?
要不要喝點酒？

中： I can't drink tonight. I'll have a meeting in the morning.
今晚我不能喝。明早我有個會議。

每課一句 3秒鐘，強化英語力！

📢 Do you take credit cards or checks?
（你們收信用卡或支票嗎？）

📢 Can I transfer my drink to my dinner tab?
（可以把酒帳算到用餐帳單上嗎？）

📢 I prefer to pay for my drinks as I go.
（我較喜歡喝多少就付多少現金。）

📢 I've got the bill.
（我請客。）

tab [tæb]

帳單

champagne [ʃæmˈpen]

香檳酒

prefer [prɪˈfɝ]

較喜歡

transfer to

轉入

ready [ˈrɛdɪ]

準備好

bar

酒吧台

When you were born, you cried and the world rejoiced. Live your life so that when you die, the world cries and you rejoice.

（出生時，你哭泣而全世界欣喜。好好過一生，這樣一來，你死時，全世界哭泣而你卻欣喜。）

食的健康

The food has a lot of fat.
這些食物有很多脂肪。

精華短句 一學就會！最簡單、迷你的會

- It seems to be greasy.
  （它似乎很油膩。）

- You know how unhealthy it can be?
  （你知道那有多麼不健康?）

- Be careful of fatty dishes here.
  （要小心這裡比較油膩的菜。）

- Have you had trouble getting low fat dishes?
  （你找低油脂食品有困難嗎？）

- The food here can have a lot of fat.
  （這裡的食物可以有很多脂肪的。）

中：	How have you been doing with the local food?	你對本地食物還習慣吧？
外：	O.K. It seems to be greasy.	還好。 本地食物似乎很油膩。
中：	Sometimes it is. You have to be careful.	有時候確實是這樣。 你要小心些才好。
外：	Actually, I like it.	事實上，我喜歡油膩。
中：	I would really be careful. The food here can have a lot of fat.	是我的話，我還是寧願小心些。 這裡的食物可以有很多脂肪的。
外：	I am sure it does.	我確定是有很多脂肪。
中：	You know how unhealthy it can be?	你知道那有多麼不健康？

| 外： | Yes.
I really should watch out. | 我知道。
我實在是須要小心些。 |

進階應用 舉一反三！聽說力更上一層樓

⊃ 警告友人小心油膩，怎麼說？

M: Be careful of the fatty dishes here.
（要小心這裡比較油膩的菜。）

W: Thanks.
（謝謝。）

I will.
（我會的。）

⊃ 警告友人小心油膩，說法二

W: Should I eat at the restaurant next door?
（我可以在隔壁的餐館用餐嗎？）

M: Yes, but I would be careful.
（可以，但若是我的話，我會小心。）

They have a lot of fatty dishes.
（他們有很多菜色很油膩。）

M: Have you had trouble getting low fat dishes here?
（你在本地找低油脂食品有困難嗎？）

W: Yes, I really do not know what to ask for.
（有困難。我不知道點些什麼菜。）

每課一句 3秒鐘，強化英語力！

🔊 You have to watch out for the fried dishes here.
（你必須注意這裡油炸的菜餚。）

🔊 Would you like me to make a list of fatty dishes to avoid?
（你要我列一張應避免的油膩菜單嗎？）

🔊 If you need help finding low fat dishes to eat, let me know.
（你若需要協助找低脂食品吃，請讓我知道。）

🔊 We should push our work; the work should not push us.
（我們應該主動工作，而非被工作推著走。）

常用單字 3秒鐘，強化單字力！

greasy [ˈgrisɪ]	油膩
seem [sim]	似乎
actually [ˈæktʃʊəlɪ]	事實上
fat	脂肪
unhealthy [ʌnˈhɛlθɪ]	不健康
watch out	注意
low fat	低脂
avoid [əˈvɔɪd]	避免

🔊 What we do willingly is easy.
（我們願意做的事情就不覺得難。）

🔊 We must not lie down and cry "God help us."
（我們不該躺著什麼都不做，只乞求上帝幫助。）

🔊 There is no labor in the labor of love, and there is love in (the) honest labor.
（做喜愛的事就不覺得苦，踏實的工作孕育出喜愛。）

🔊 What is learned in the cradle is carried to the grave.
（幼時所學的東西會帶入墳墓。）

🔊 A young idler, an old beggar.
（少壯不努力，老大徒傷悲。）

🔊 Age is honorable and youth is noble.
（長者可敬，少者可貴。）

🔊 Youth does not mind where it sets its foot.
（年輕人不介意從何處起步。）

🔊 Every man is his own worst enemy.
（人生最大的敵人是自己。）

Chapter 5

休閒英語

邀請參加宴會

There is a party tonight at my house.

今晚我家有個宴會。

- What are you doing this weekend?
  （這個週末，你要做什麼事？）

- There is a party.
  （有個宴會。）

- It sounds like fun.
  （聽起來好像很好玩。）

- I was not invited.
  （我沒受到邀請。）

- I would love to go.
  （我很想去。）

- We are having a small party tonight.
  （我們今晚有個小宴會。）

- Are you invited?
  （你有沒有受到邀請？）

實況會話 靈活運用！會話、聽力同步加強

外：	What are you doing this weekend?	這個週末，你有什麼事？
中：	There is a party tomorrow night at Mike's house.	明晚在麥克家有個宴會。
外：	It sounds like fun.	聽起來好像很好玩的樣子。
中：	You should come.	你應該來參加。
外：	I was not invited.	我又沒收到邀請。
中：	Mike told me to ask you, but I have not had the chance yet.	麥克要我邀你，但我還沒機會通知你。
外：	I would love to go. Where does he live?	我很想去。他住哪？
中：	I can pick you up if it is easier.	我可以用車接你，那比較容易一些。
外：	Sounds like an even better plan!	那可更是個好主意。

⊃ 邀請參加宴會，怎麼說？

M: **We are having a small party tonight.**
（我們今晚有個小宴會。）

Would you like to come?
（妳要來嗎？）

W: **No, I cannot.**
（不，我不能來。）

I have to finish this proposal.
（我得將這份企畫做完。）

⊃ 感謝別人邀請的說法

M: **Did you hear about the office party today after work?**
（妳聽說今天下班公司有個宴會嗎？）

W: **No.**
（我不知道。）

Thanks for telling me.
（謝謝你告訴我。）

⊃ 答應參加宴會的說法

M: **Would you like to come to the party tonight?**
（妳今晚要來參加宴會嗎？）

W: **Yes. That would be great!**
（好啊。能參加，太好了。）

📢 **每課一句** 3秒鐘，強化英語力！

🔊 I am having a party. I would like you to come.
（我要舉行一個宴會。我邀你來參加。）

🔊 I am having a party. Would you like to come?
（我要舉行一個宴會。你要來嗎？）

🔊 Has Mike already invited you to the party?
（麥克邀請你來參加宴會了沒有？）

📢 **常用單字** 3秒鐘，強化單字力！

weekend [ˈwikˈɛnd]	週末
already [ɔlˈrɛdɪ]	已經
invite [ɪnˈvaɪt]	邀請
pick up	（用車）接
easier [ˈizɪɚ]	容易些
finish [ˈfɪnəʃ]	完成
proposal [prəˈpozl̩]	企畫

宴會上的對話

I am having a good time.
我玩得很盡興。

精華短句 一學就會！最簡單、迷你的會話

- Great party, huh?
  （很成功的舞會，不是嗎？）

- Sounds neat.
  （聽起來滿好。）

- Would you like me to get you another drink?
  （要不要我再給你拿杯飲料？）

- Are you having a good time?
  （你玩得盡興嗎？）

- Have you met John?
  （你見過約翰嗎？）

- I really like the way this party is set up.
  （我很喜歡這個宴會的佈置。）

- Did you drive here or get a ride?
  （你開車來還是搭別人的車？）

實況會話 靈活運用！會話、聽力同步加強

中：	Great party, huh?	很成功的舞會，不是嗎？
外：	Yes. I am having a good time.	是的。 我玩得很盡興。
中：	Did you see how they decorated the dance area?	你有沒有看見他們怎麼佈置舞池？
外：	No, what did they do?	沒注意，他們怎麼做？
中：	They ran streamers all along the edges of the ceiling.	他們沿著天花板邊繞彩帶。
外：	Sounds neat.	聽起來不賴。
中：	Would you like me to get you another drink?	要不要我再給你拿杯飲料？
外：	Yes, please do.	好，麻煩你。

⊃ 問別人是否盡興，怎麼說？

M: Are you having a good time?
（妳玩得盡興嗎？）

W: Yes, I just feel awkward because I do not know anyone.
（盡興。不過我覺得彆扭，因為不認識半個人。）

⊃ 介紹朋友認識的說法

M: Have you met Sam?
（你見過山姆嗎？）

W: No.
（沒有。）

Hello, Sam.
（你好，山姆。）

Do you work at the company?
（你也在我們公司上班嗎？）

⊃ 讚美宴會場的說法

M: I really like the way this party is set up.
（我很喜歡這個宴會的佈置。）

W: Yes, me too.
（是的，我也是。）

It is very open.
（它佈置得很寬敞。）

每課一句 3秒鐘，強化英語力！

📢 Did you get here all right?
（你找到這裡沒有什麼困難吧？）

📢 Did you drive here or get a ride?
（你開車來還是搭別人的車？）

📢 Have you seen Mike?
（你有沒有看見麥克？）

📢 Can I get you anything?
（你要不要我幫你拿點什麼東西？）

常用單字 3秒鐘，強化單字力！

decorate ['dɛkəret]	裝飾
streamer ['strimɚ]	彩帶
ceiling ['silɪŋ]	天花板
awkward ['ɔkwɚd]	彆扭

📢 Experience keeps a dear school.
（經驗是最佳教育。）

Chapter 5

休閒英語

191

參觀球賽

I am going to the baseball game.
我要去看棒球賽。

精華短句　一學就會！最簡單、迷你的會話

- Let's go see a ball game.
  （我們去看場球賽。）

- It is a lot of fun.
  （那是很好玩的。）

- I have never been to a game here.
  （我在這裡還沒看過球賽。）

- Not at all.
  （不會的。）

- I did not mean to make trouble.
  （我不是要讓你添麻煩的。）

- What are the ball games like here?
  （這裡的球賽精彩嗎？）

- You ought to come with me.
  （你應該跟我一道去。）

實況會話 靈活運用！會話、聽力同步加強

外：	What are you doing tonight?	你今晚要做什麼？
中：	I am going to the baseball game. Would you like to come?	我要去看棒球賽。 你要不要去？
外：	I have never been to a game here.	我在這裡還沒看過球賽呢！
中：	It is a lot of fun.	很好玩的。
外：	I would love to go.	我想去。
中：	Great. I will buy an extra ticket.	很好。 我會多買一張票。
外：	Oh, I did not mean to make trouble.	哎呀，我不是要麻煩你的。
中：	Not at all. The tickets are no problem to get.	不麻煩。 買票不是問題。

Chapter 5

休閒英語

⊃ 邀請去看球賽，怎麼說？

W: Have you seen any of the ball games here?
（你在這裡看過球賽嗎？）

M: No.
（沒有。）

But I would like to go.
（但我很想去。）

⊃ 邀請去看球賽，說法二

M: I was wondering if you would like to come to the ball game with me tomorrow.
（我在想，妳明天要不要與我一道去看球賽？）

W: I can not.
（我不能去。）

Can we go another time?
（可以另外擇期再去嗎？）

⊃ 乘機邀請去看球賽

W: What are the ball games like here?
（這裡的球賽怎樣？）

M: They are a lot of fun.
（球賽很好玩。）

You ought to come with me sometime.
（你幾時應該跟我一起去看。）

每課一句 3秒鐘，強化英語力！

📢 There is a ball game tonight.
（今晚有場球賽。）

📢 Do you want to go?
（你要去嗎？）

📢 Do you like ball games?
（你喜歡球賽嗎？）

📢 Let's go see a ball game tonight.
（今晚我們去看場球賽吧。）

常用單字 3秒鐘，強化單字力！

baseball	棒球
ought to	應該
sometime ['sʌm'taɪm]	某個時候
would like to	想要

📢 The man who loses his opportunities loses himself.
（失去機會的人，就是失去了自己。）

Unit 38

看電影

Why don't we go see a movie?
我們何不去看場電影？

精華短句 一學就會！最簡單、迷你的會話

- Like what?
  （舉個例子吧？）

- Let's forget about it.
  （我們就不要再提了吧。）

- There is a lot of new stuff to see.
  （有很多新東西可以看。）

- Have you seen the new action movie?
  （你看過那部新動作片沒有？）

🔊 He is only bright that shines by himself.
（唯有靠自己發光的人，才能真正明亮。）

實況會話 靈活運用！會話、聽力同步加強

中：	I hope you have not been bored since you have been here.	希望你自從來到此地，不會覺得很無聊。
外：	Not at all. There is a lot of new stuff to see.	不會的。有很多新東西可以看。
中：	There is a lot that is the same, too.	也有很多看來看去都一樣的。
外：	Like what?	比如哪些東西？
中：	Let's forget about the boring stuff. We have nice movie theaters.	咱們別提無聊的東西。 我們有很好的電影院。
外：	I have not seen a movie in a long time.	我好久沒看電影了。
中：	Why don't we go see one tonight?	我們今晚何不去看場電影？
外：	Great!	好極了。

Chapter 5

休閒英語

➲ 邀請去看電影，怎麼說？

M: Have you seen the new action movie?
（你看過那部新動作片沒有？）

W: No. I would like to go see it.
（沒有。我想去看。）

➲ 邀請去看電影，說法二

M: Would you like to see a movie tonight?
（妳晚上要不要去看場電影？）

W: Yes, that would be fun.
（好，那一定很有意思。）

➲ 邀請去看電影，說法三

W: If you don't have plans, why don't we see a movie tonight?
（你要是沒有特別計畫，咱們今晚何不去看場電影？）

M: Sounds like a good plan!
（聽起來像是個好主意噢！）

🔊 Experience must be bought.
（必須付出代價學到經驗。）

每課一句 3秒鐘，強化英語力！

◀» Let's see a movie tonight.
（咱們今晚去看場電影吧。）

◀» If you are getting bored, we can go see a movie.
（你要是覺得無聊，咱們去看場電影吧。）

◀» Do you like to go to the movies?
（你要不要去看電影？）

◀» I hope this will be a good movie.
（我希望這會是部好電影。）

◀» That was a great film. I would see it again!
（那是一部好電影。我會想再看一次。）

常用單字 3秒鐘，強化單字力！

movie ['muvɪ]	電影
stuff [stʌf]	東西
theater ['θɪətɚ]	戲院
film [fɪlm]	電影

◀» Kind words soften anger.
（好聽的話使怒氣緩和。）

Chapter 5

休閒英語

199

參加音樂會

There is a concert tonight.
今晚有場音樂會。

精華短句 一學就會！最簡單、迷你的會話

- Do you like to go to concerts?
  （你要不要去聽音樂會？）

- There is a concert tonight at the stadium.
  （今晚體育場有音樂會。）

- It is supposed to be a good group.
  （那應該是個很好的樂團。）

- It has been a long time.
  （好久啦。）

- I don't want to go by myself.
  （我不願獨自一人去。）

- Pleasure comes through toil.
  （苦盡甘來。）

實況會話 靈活運用！會話、聽力同步加強

中：	Do you have plans tonight?	今晚有何計畫？
外：	No. Why?	沒有啊。 為何有此一問呢？
中：	There is a concert tonight at the stadium.	今晚體育場有音樂會。
外：	Oh. Are you going?	是嗎？你要去嗎？
中：	I thought about it. I wanted to see if you wanted to go.	我有想過要去。 我想看看你去不去。
外：	Yes, I think it would be a good time.	好啊，我想可以玩得很愉快。
中：	It is supposed to be a good group.	那應該是個很好的樂團。

進階應用 舉一反三！聽說力更上一層樓

➲ 表示很久沒有參加音樂會的說法

M: Do you like to go to concerts?
（你要不要去聽音樂會？）

Chapter 5

休閒英語

W: Yes.
（好。）

It has been a long time since I have been to one.
（離我上次參加音樂會至今，已經很久了。）

邀人一起去音樂會

W: What are you doing tonight?
（你今晚要做什麼？）

M: Actually, I was just about to ask you if you wanted to go to a concert.
（事實上，我正要問你是否要去聽音樂會呢？）

不想獨自做某事，怎麼說？

M: Have you heard about the concert tonight?
（你聽說過今晚的音樂會嗎？）

W: Yes.
（是的。）

I want to go, but I don't want to go by my-self.
（我想參加，但我不願獨自一人去。）

問人去過音樂會沒有？

M: Have you been to a concert here?
（你在本地參加過音樂會嗎？）

W: **No.**
（沒有。）

What are they like here?
（這裡的音樂會好嗎？）

每課一句 3秒鐘，強化英語力！

◆》 **This group is supposed to be really good.**
（這一團應該很好才對。）

◆》 **I have never heard this group play before.**
（我沒聽過這團演奏過。）

◆》 **It sure is crowded!**
（真的好擠噢！）

◆》 **Do you have a seating preference for the concert?**
（你去音樂會有沒有比較喜歡坐哪邊？）

常用單字 3秒鐘，強化單字力！

concert [ˈkɑnsɚt]	音樂會	
stadium [ˈstedɪəm]	體育場	
preference [ˈprɛfərəns]	偏好	
suppose [səˈpoz]	假定	

參加百老匯歌舞劇

The show is sold out.
這場表演的票賣光了。

精華短句 一學就會！最簡單、迷你的會話

- Have you ever seen a Broadway show?
  （你看過百老匯歌舞劇嗎？）

- Do you enjoy the show?
  （你喜歡這個表演嗎？）

- I have four reserved in my name.
  （我用我的名字預訂四張票。）

- Maybe next time.
  （也許下回吧。）

- This show has gotten great reviews.
  （這個表演有不錯的評論。）

- I hope the show is not sold out.
  （我希望這場表演的票不會賣光。）

實況會話 靈活運用！會話、聽力同步加強

外：	Have you ever seen a Broadway show?	你看過百老匯歌舞劇嗎？
中：	Yes, I have seen several.	有，我看過幾部。
外：	Do you enjoy them?	你喜歡它們嗎？
中：	Oh yes!	啊，是的。
外：	There is one playing tomorrow night if you want to go.	你如果想去的話，明晚有一場表演。
中：	That sounds great. Do you already have tickets?	那太好了。你已經有票了嗎？
外：	No, but I have four reserved in my name.	沒有，但我用我的名字預訂四張。

He that can't endure the bad will not live to see the good.
（無法撐過苦境，無法看到美地。）

⊃ 婉拒別人的邀請

M: Do you want to see the Broadway show with us?
（你要不要和我們一起看百老匯歌舞劇。）

W: No, I cannot.
（不，我不能去。）

Maybe next time.
（也許下回吧。）

⊃ 討論表演的說法

M: This show has gotten great reviews.
（這個表演的評論不錯。）

W: Really? I have not had a chance to read them.
真的？我還沒讀到評論。

⊃ 在票房口的對話

M: I hope the show is not sold out.
（我希望這場表演的票不會賣光。）

W: I know.
（我知道你的意思。）

The line looks really long.
（買票的隊看起來很長。）

每課一句 3秒鐘，強化英語力！

🔊 Have you heard of the show downtown tonight?
（你聽說過今晚在市中心的表演嗎？）

🔊 I am excited about seeing this show.
（對於看這場表演，我很興奮。）

🔊 This is a new show, so I hope it will be good.
（這是一齣新戲，我希望它還好。）

常用單字 3秒鐘，強化單字力！

Broadway show	百老匯歌舞劇
reserve [rɪˈzɝv]	預訂；預約
review [rɪˈvju]	評論
sold out	售罄
line [laɪn]	隊伍

參加文化活動

What should I wear?
我應該穿什麼衣著？

精華短句 一學就會！最簡單、迷你的會話

- Would you like to come?
  （你要來參加嗎？）

- I have heard about it.
  （我聽說過了。）

- I did not want to go alone.
  （我不要獨自去。）

- Why don't you come with me?
  （你何不跟我一起去？）

- They are spectacular.
  （它們是很壯觀的。）

實況會話 靈活運用！會話、聽力同步加強

外：	There is a charity ball this weekend.	本週末有個慈善舞會。
中：	I had heard something about it.	我稍微有聽說過。
外：	Are you going to go?	你去不去？
中：	I did not want to go alone.	我不要獨自去。
外：	Why don't you come with me?	你何不跟我一起去？
中：	That would be great. What should I wear?	那太好了。我該穿什麼服裝？
外：	Semi-formal attire.	半正式打扮。
中：	All right.	好吧。

📢 You never know what you can do till you try.
（試了你才知道自己的能耐。）

Chapter 5

休閒英語

⊃ 問人家是否要參加某種活 ？

M: Would you like to come to the arts festival this weekend?
（你這個週末要不要參加「藝術祭」？）

W: Yes. Are you going, too?
（要。你也要去嗎？）

⊃ 表示很好看的說法

M: Have you seen any of the festival parades here?
（你看過這裡節慶的遊行沒有？）

W: No, but I have heard they are spectacular!
（沒有，但我聽說遊行很壯觀。）

⊃ 感謝對方邀請的說法

M: I am going to the play in the park tonight.
（我今晚要去公園看戲劇。）

Do you want to go?
（你要去嗎？）

W: Yes, thanks for asking.
（好啊，謝謝你邀請。）

每課一句 3秒鐘，強化英語力！

🔊 Do you know about the festival?
（你知道這個節慶嗎？）

🔊 Have you been to the museum exhibit yet?
（你去看過博物館展覽沒有？）

🔊 Do you want to see the museum exhibition?
（你要不要去看博物館的展覽？）

🔊 If you want a ride to the play, let me know.
（你若須要我載你去看戲，就告訴我。）

常用單字 3秒鐘，強化單字力！

charity ['tʃærətɪ]	慈善
ball	舞會
festival ['fɛstəvəl]	節慶
parade [pə'red]	遊行
spectacular [spɛk'tækjələ]	壯觀的
exhibit [ɪg'zɪbɪt]	展覽

🔊 He who risks nothing gains nothing.
（不入虎穴，焉得虎子。）

Chapter 5

休閒英語

上休閒酒吧

There is a nice bar nearby.
附近有間好酒吧。

精華短句 一學就會！最簡單、迷你的會話

- Do you want to go get a drink?
  （你要不要去喝一杯？）

- Where at?
  （位於哪裡？）

- Where is a good place to have a drink?
  （哪裡是喝酒的好地方？）

- There is a nice lounge nearby.
  （附近有一家好雅座酒吧。）

- Where is a good place to relax?
  （哪裡是放鬆身心的好地方？）

- Would you like to come the lounge for drinks?
  （要不要去雅座酒吧喝酒？）

實況會話 靈活運用！會話、聽力同步加強

外：	What are you doing after work?	下班後做什麼？
中：	I do not have any plans.	我沒有特別計畫。
外：	Do you want to go get a drink?	要不要去喝一杯？
中：	Sounds great. Where at?	聽起來像個好主意。上哪裡？
外：	There is a nice piano bar nearby.	附近有間好鋼琴酒吧。
中：	Is the piano player good?	彈鋼琴的琴藝好嗎？
外：	No worse than anywhere else.	不會比別地方差。

🔊 You never know till you tried.
（不試不知。）

Chapter 5

休閒英語

⊃ 邀請人上鋼琴酒吧，怎麼說？

M: Have you been to the new piano bar?
（你去過那家新鋼琴酒吧嗎？）

W: No.
（還沒。）

I had thought about going after work today.
（我曾經想過今晚下班去。）

⊃ 問有沒有地方休閒喝酒？

W: Where is a good place to have a drink and relax?
（哪裡是喝酒和放鬆身心的好地方？）

M: There is a nice lounge across town.
（本市的另一區有一家好雅座酒吧。）

⊃ 要對方等一下，拿衣服的說法

M: Would you like to come with us to the lounge for drinks?
（要不要與我們一道去酒吧喝酒？）

W: Yes. Just let me get my coat.
（好啊。讓我拿一下外套。）

每課一句 3秒鐘，強化英語力！

🔊 I have heard the piano player sings too.
（我有聽說這位鋼琴師也會唱歌。）

🔊 I really like the piano music.
（我真的喜歡這支鋼琴曲。）

🔊 The bar has a nice atmosphere.
（這間酒吧氣氛很好。）

🔊 These chairs are comfortable after a hard day.
（一整天累下來，這些椅子坐起來真舒服。）

常用單字 3秒鐘，強化單字力！

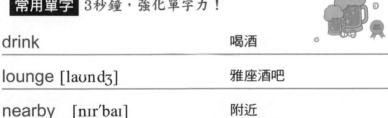

drink	喝酒
lounge [laʊndʒ]	雅座酒吧
nearby [nɪrˈbaɪ]	附近
worse [wɝs]	更糟
relax [rɪˈlæks]	放鬆身心
atmosphere [ˈætməsfɪr]	氣氛
comfortable [ˈkʌmfətəbl̩]	舒適
across town	都市的另一端

上博物館

The museum is beautiful.
博物館真漂亮。

44

精華短句 一學就會！最簡單、迷你的會話

- Do you like art?
  （你喜歡藝術嗎？）

- I am not in the mood.
  （我沒那個心情。）

- The museum here is beautiful.
  （本地的博物館很漂亮。）

- How about Saturday?
  （約在星期六，你看如何？）

- I have wanted to see it for some time.
  （我好久以來就想去參觀了。）

- My favorite kind of art is Chinese painting.
  （我最喜歡的藝術是中國國畫。）

實況會話 靈活運用！會話、聽力同步加強

中：	Do you like art?	你喜歡藝術嗎？
外：	Sometimes. I have to be in the mood.	有時候吧。 我得要心情好時 才喜歡。
中：	The museum here is beautiful.	這裡的博物館可 是很漂亮噢。
外：	I would love to see it.	我很想去看。
中：	Why don't we go this weekend?	我們何不這個週 末去？
外：	O.K. How about Saturday?	好啊。 星期六如何？
中：	Great. What time do you want to go?	很好。 你幾點要去？
外：	Probably about 10:00 A.M.	大約早上十點左 右吧。

◁ Between two stools you fall to the ground.
（腳踏雙凳必墜地。）

Chapter 5

休閒英語

⊃ 向對方表示有興趣到某處的說法

M: Have you been to the museum here?
（你曾經到過本地的博物館嗎？）

W: No. I would like to go, though.
（沒有。不過我想去的。）

⊃ 表示已經想很久要到某地，怎麼說？

M: I am going to the museum.
（我正要去博物館。）

Would you like to go?
（你要不要去？）

W: Yes.
（好啊。）

I have wanted to see it for some time.
（我想去參觀已經有好一段時間了。）

⊃ 問有沒有博物館的問法

W: Do you have a museum here?
（你們這裡有沒有博物館？）

M: Yes.
（有。）

We have a large museum downtown.
（我們市中心有一間大博物館。）

每課一句 3秒鐘，強化英語力！

🔊 Do you want to go to the museum?
（你要不要去博物館？）

🔊 Do you like sculpture or paintings better?
（你比較喜歡雕刻還是繪畫？）

🔊 Have you ever done any painting?
（你有沒有做過繪畫？）

🔊 What is your favorite kind of art?
（你最喜歡的藝術是什麼？）

常用單字 3秒鐘，強化單字力！

mood [mud]	心情
museum [mjuˈzɪəm]	博物館
beautiful [ˈbjutəfəl]	美麗的
sculpture [ˈskʌlptʃɚ]	雕塑
painting [ˈpentɪŋ]	繪畫
favorite kind of ~	最喜愛的～種類

Chapter 5

休閒英語

219

參觀特別展覽

I cannot wait to see the exhibit.
我等不及要看這個展覽。

45

精華短句 一學就會！最簡單、迷你的會話

- I have thought about getting tickets.
  （我曾想過買票去看。）

- I like to go with other people.
  （我喜歡和別人一道去。）

- I like to get other people's perspective.
  （我喜歡聽別人的看法。）

- If you want to come, you are welcome.
  （假如你想來，歡迎得很。）

- The exhibit is fantastic.
  （這個展覽太棒了！）

🔊 If you run after two hares, you will catch neither.
（同時追兩兔，兩頭都落空。）

實況會話 靈活運用！會話、聽力同步加強

中：	There is a great Egyptian exhibit coming to town soon.	不久即將有個很好的埃及特展到本地來。
外：	Really?	真的？
中：	Yes, I have thought about getting tickets.	是的，我想過要買票去參觀。
外：	How much are they?	票價是多少？
中：	I don't know, but I can tell you when they come in.	我不知道，不過買到票時，我就可以告訴你。
外：	That would be nice.	那很好。
中：	If you like, I can buy them and we can go together.	你喜歡的話，我可以買票，然後我們一起去參觀。
外：	Good. I like to go with other people and get their perspective.	好。我喜歡和別人一起去，聽聽別人的看法。

⤵ 當別人提出邀請時的其他回答法

M: Do you want to see the Japanese exhibit?
（你要不要去參觀日本特展？）

W: I did not even know there is one!
（我根本不知道有這項展覽！）

⤵ 提出邀請的其他說法

M: We are going to see the Egyptian exhibit.
（我們要去看埃及特展。）

If you want to come, you are welcome.
（你要一起去看的話，很歡迎。）

W: That sounds like a lot of fun.
（那聽起來像很有意思的樣子。）

⤵ 問展覽性質，怎麼說？

W: Have you seen the exhibit downtown?
（你看過市中心的展覽沒有？）

M: No, what is there?
（沒有，是什麼展覽？）

🔊 Adversity leads to prosperity.
（逆境導致成功。）

每課一句 3秒鐘，強化英語力！

🔊 This is a world class exhibit.
（這是一項世界級的展覽。）

🔊 The paper says the exhibit is fantastic.
（報紙說這個展覽非常好。）

🔊 I cannot wait to see the exhibit.
（我等不及要去看這項展覽。）

🔊 Have you seen the exhibit before?
（你以前看過這個展覽嗎？）

常用單字 3秒鐘，強化單字力！

Egyptian [ɪˈdʒɪpʃən]		埃及的
coming to town		來到本地
perspective [pɚˈspɛktɪv]		見解
fantastic [fænˈtæstɪk]		與眾不同
welcome [ˈwɛlkəm]		歡迎
world class		世界級

🔊 No cross, no crown.
（沒有痛苦十字架，哪來榮耀冠冕。）

🔊 You can't sell the cow and drink the milk.
（魚與熊掌不可兼得。）

🔊 A man can't do two things at once.
（一心不可二用。）

🔊 A man cannot spin and reel at the same time.
（一個人不能同時紡紗又捲線。）

🔊 Don't count your chickens before they are hatched.
（勿打如意算盤。）

🔊 Slow and steady/sure wins the race.
（穩紮穩打，永操勝券。）

🔊 The best is the enemy of the good.
（「最好」是「好」的敵人。）

🔊 Better an egg today than a hen tomorrow.
（今日的一顆雞蛋，勝過明天的一隻雞。）

🔊 You can't have it both ways.
（事難兩全。）

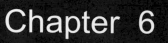

Chapter 6

商業友誼英語

協助安排住宿

Do you want to stay close by?
你要不要住近一點？

精華短句 一學就會！最簡單、迷你的會話

- Did you have a good flight in?
  （你這趟飛行還好吧？）

- I slept most of the way.
  （我大部份旅程都在睡覺。）

- This was a last-minute trip.
  （這是到最後一分鐘才成行。）

- Do you want to stay close by?
  （你要住近一點嗎？）

- Let's look close by first.
  （我們先從近一點的開始找。）

- I have no idea where I am going to stay!
  （我不知道要住哪呢！）

- Do you want a large or small room?
  （你要大房間還是小房間？）

實況會話 靈活運用！會話、聽力同步加強

中：	Did you have a good flight in?	你這趟飛行還好吧？
外：	Yes, I slept most of the way.	是的，我大部份旅程都在睡覺。
中：	Good. Do you have a hotel?	那好。 訂飯店了沒有？
外：	No. This was a last minute trip.	沒有。 這趟出差是到最後一分鐘才成行。
中：	I will be glad to help you find a place.	我很樂意幫你找個住宿的地方。
外：	I would really appreciate it.	我很感激。
中：	Do you want to stay close by, or downtown?	你要住近一點，還是住市中心？
外：	Let's look close by first.	我們先從近一點的開始找吧。

⊃ 告訴別人，還沒有找到飯店的說法

W: I have no idea where I am going to stay!
（我還不知道要住哪呢！）

M: Don't worry.
（別擔心。）

I can help you find a place.
（我可以幫你找個地方。）

⊃ 自願幫對方找住宿飯店

M: Do you need help finding a hotel?
（你需要幫忙找飯店嗎？）

W: Please.
（是的。）

I have no idea what is around.
（我不知道附近有什麼飯店。）

⊃ 感謝對方幫找飯店的其他說法

M: Relax, and I will find you a hotel for your stay.
（放心，我會幫你找飯店住的。）

W: Thanks, you are a life saver!
（謝謝，你真是救了我的命。）

每課一句 3秒鐘，強化英語力！

🔊 If you need help getting a hotel, let me know.
（假如你需要協助找飯店，就告訴我。）

🔊 Let me call around and find you a hotel.
（我打打電話，幫你找間飯店。）

🔊 Do you want a large or small room?
（你要大房間還是小房間？）

🔊 Do you need to be in a particular part of town?
（你要指定在市裡的那個特別區域嗎？）

常用單字 3秒鐘，強化單字力！

flight [flaɪt]	飛行
slept [slɛpt]	睡覺（sleep的過去式）
hotel [hoˈtɛl]	飯店；旅館
last minute	最後才決定的
appreciate [əˈpriʃɪˌet]	感激
idea [aɪˈdiə]	概念
saver [ˈsevɚ]	救命者
particular [pɚˈtɪkjələ]	特定的

建立當地公共關係

I need to get my name out.
我必須將名字傳播出去。

精華短句　一學就會！最簡單、迷你的會話

- Have you gotten settled in?
  （你可以適應了嗎？）

- The jet-lag has worn off.
  （時差比較消褪了。）

- I need to get my name out.
  （我必須將名字傳播出去。）

- That would be fantastic.
  （那太好了！）

- I would really appreciate it.
  （我將會感激不盡。）

- That would be a big help.
  （你真是幫了我一個大忙。）

實況會話 靈活運用！會話、聽力同步加強

中：	Have you gotten settled in?	你比較可以適應了嗎？
外：	Yes. The jet-lag has worn off.	是的。 時差比較不那麼累了。
中：	What are your plans?	你計畫怎麼做？
外：	I need to get my name out there to the local businesses.	我必須把我的名字傳播到本地的商圈。
中：	My cousin is an advertising agent. He knows lots of people. Do you want me to have him call you?	我表親是廣告商。 他認識很多朋友。 你要我叫他打電話給你嗎？
外：	That would be fantastic.	那太好了。
中：	I will call him this morning and set up an appointment for you.	我今天早上會給他打電話，幫你跟他約個時間。
外：	Thanks a lot!	多謝了。

Chapter 6

商業友誼英語

231

⊃ 要對方幫忙建立人脈的說法

W: Do you know anyone in town who can help me get started?
（你在本地認識什麼人可以幫我踏出第一步嗎？）

M: Yes. Let me make some calls.
（有的。讓我打幾個電話。）

⊃ 感謝對方協助建立關係

M: If you give me your resume, I can fax it to several people around town.
（要是妳把妳的履歷表給我，我可以傳真給本地的幾個人。）

W: That would be a big help.
你真是幫了我一個大忙。

⊃ 希望對方幫忙約朋友見面

M: I know someone downtown who can help you with your advertising.
（我認識幾個人在市中心，他們可以幫你做廣告。）

W: I would really appreciate it if you could set up that appointment.
（要是你能幫我同他們約個時間見面，我是感激不盡。）

每課一句 3秒鐘，強化英語力！

🔊 Would you like me to call around for you?
（你要我幫你打幾個電話嗎？）

🔊 Are you looking to meet anyone specific?
（你有沒有要特別與什麼人見面？）

🔊 I can make some calls for you, if you like.
（你願意的話，我可以幫你打幾個電話。）

🔊 Let me know when you are ready,
and I will introduce you to some business
associates.
（你準備好就通知我，我要介紹幾個商業伙伴給你認識。）

常用單字 3秒鐘，強化單字力！

settle [ˈsɛtl̩]	平息；解決
jet-lag	（旅遊）時差
worn off	消褪
cousin [ˈkʌzn̩]	表（堂）兄弟姊妹
advertise [ˈædvɚˌtaɪz]	廣告
agent [ˈedʒənt]	代理人
resume [ˈrɛzʊˌme]	履歷表

Chapter 6

商業友誼英語

233

fax	傳真
set up	訂立
appointment [əˈpɔɪntmənt]	約會
specific [spɪˈsɪfɪk]	特定的
introduce [ɪntrəˈdjus]	介紹
associate [əˈsoʃɪ͵et]	伙伴

🔊 Don't cross a bridge till you come to it.
（船到橋頭自然直。）

🔊 Don't worry for tomorrow.
（不要為明天憂慮。）

🔊 Come what may, heaven won't fall.
（無論怎樣，天空都不會掉下來。）

交通工具

I would rent a car.
我會選擇租車。

精華短句 一學就會！最簡單、迷你的會話

- How are you planning to get around the province?
  （你打算如何在本省行 ？）

- I do not know yet.
  （我還不知道。）

- Not really.
  （不是。）

- Do you have a way to get around town?
  （你在市裡行動，有沒有辦法？）

- I need help to find transportation.
  （我需要協助找交通工具。）

- Where would I get one?
  （去哪裡可以弄到一個？）

中：	How are you planning to get around the province?	你打算如何在本省行動？
外：	I do not know yet.	我還不知道。
中：	You can take the train. Sometimes that will not get you to where you want to go, though.	你可以搭火車。不過有時火車無法讓你去你想去的地方。
外：	What do you think I should do?	你認為我該怎麼做？
中：	I would rent a car.	我會選擇租車。
外：	Where would I get one?	到哪裡可以租車呢？
中：	I can take you to a couple of rental agencies today.	我今天帶你去幾個租車的地方。

🔊 Don't waste life in doubts and fears.
（生命不要浪費在猜疑和恐懼中。）

進階應用 舉一反三！聽說力更上一層樓

⟶ 問對方有沒有交通工具的問法

M: Do you have a way to get around town?
（你在市裡行動，有沒有辦法？）

W: Not really.
（沒有。）

I am just using the subway.
（我都坐地鐵。）

⟶ 要求幫忙找交通工具

M: I need help to find transportation.
（我需要協助找交通工具。）

W: I will help you.
（我會幫你的。）

⟶ 要求幫忙找交通工具，說法二

W: What should I do about getting around town?
（我該怎麼辦才能順利在市裡行 ？）

M: I can help you find a car.
（我可以幫你找部車。）

◀ Can you afford to rent a car?
（你能付得起錢租車嗎？）

◀ Would you rather buy a car?
（你寧願買車嗎？）

◀ Would you like me to get you a taxi?
（你要不要我幫你叫計程車？）

◀ Do you know where to get the train tickets?
（你知道在哪裡買火車票嗎？）

get around	在附近行動
a couple of	一些
rental agency	租車公司
transportation [ˌtrænspɚˈteʃən]	交通（工具）
afford to	付得起錢

◀ He who leaves the fame of good works after him does not die.
（生前做好事，死後留名聲。）

Chapter 7

關懷朋友英語

醫療保健

Are you feeling O.K.?
你覺得不舒服嗎？

精華短句 一學就會！最簡單、迷你的會話

- Are you feeling O.K.?
  （你覺得不舒服嗎？）

- Are you not feeling well?
  （你覺得不舒服嗎？）

- I have had a bad cough.
  （我咳得很厲害。）

- It keeps getting worse.
  （它越來越嚴重。）

- Have you been to a doctor?
  （你去看過醫生了嗎？）

- What doctor do you go to?
  （你都看那位醫生？）

- If you don't feel well, go home.
  （你要是不舒服，就回家吧。）

實況會話 靈活運用！會話、聽力同步加強

中：	Are you feeling O.K.?	你覺得不舒服嗎？
外：	No, I have had a cough, and it keeps getting worse.	不舒服。我咳得厲害，而且越來越嚴重。
中：	Have you been to a doctor?	你去看過醫生了嗎？
外：	I do not know where to see one.	我不知道去哪裡看醫生。
中：	I will be happy to take you to a clinic.	我很樂意帶你去診所。
外：	I would really appreciate it.	謝謝你。
中：	I will show you the hospital too, just so you know where it is.	我也會指大醫院給你看，以便你知道醫院在哪裡。

◀》 Misery shows the man what he is.
（災難使人露出本性。）

關懷朋友英語

⊃ 願協助找醫生的說法

M: Do you need help finding a doctor?
（你需要協助找醫生嗎？）

W: Yes. I don't know the town that well yet.
（需要。因我對本市還不很熟。）

⊃ 願幫忙跟醫生掛號的說法

W: What doctor do you go to?
（你都看那位醫生？）

M: The company doctor.
（公司內部自己的醫生。）

I can make you an appointment if you like.
（你要的話，我可以幫你掛號。）

⊃ 建議朋友不舒服就回家

M: If you don't feel well, go home.
（你要是不舒服，就回家吧。）

W: Thanks, I will.
（謝謝，我會的。）

◀》 No pleasure without pain.
（沒有苦，就沒有樂。）

每課一句 3秒鐘，強化英語力！

📢 Do you prefer a male or female doctor?
（你比較喜歡看男醫生還是女醫生？）

📢 Have you been to the public health clinic?
（你去過公共衛生所沒有？）

📢 You need a prescription to buy this drug.
（你需要處方才能買這種藥。）

常用單字 3秒鐘，強化單字力！

cough [kɔf]	咳嗽
hospital ['hɑspətəl]	大型醫院
male [mel]	男
female ['fimel]	女
clinic ['klɪnɪk]	診所
prescription [prɪs'krɪpʃən]	（醫藥）處方
drug [drʌg]	藥物

📢 Once a man and twice a child.
（當一次成人，當兩次小孩。）

精華短句 一學就會！最簡單、迷你的會話

- Isn't today your birthday?
  （今天不是你的生日嗎？）

- Happy Birthday!
  （祝你生日快樂！）

- I want to wish you a happy birthday.
  （我要祝妳生日快樂。）

- That is very nice of you.
  （你太好了。）

- I am flattered that you remembered.
  （你記得我的生日，我真受寵若驚。）

- I do get lonely.
  （我真的感到孤單。）

實況會話 靈活運用！會話、聽力同步加強

中：	Isn't today your birthday?	今天不是你的生日嗎？
外：	Yes, it is.	是的。
中：	Happy Birthday!	祝你生日快樂。
外：	Thanks. I am flattered that you remembered.	謝了。 你記得我的生日，我真受寵若驚。
中：	Why don't you come over to my house tonight for dinner?	你何不到我家來吃晚飯？
外：	That would be very nice.	那太好了。
中：	I know it must be hard being away from your family.	我知道離開你的家人，一定很難過的。
外：	Sometimes I do get lonely.	有時候，我真的會感到孤單。

⊃「生日快樂」的說法

M: I just wanted to wish you a happy birthday.
（我要祝妳生日快樂。）

W: Oh, thanks.
（噢，謝謝。）

I can't believe you remembered!
（真不敢相信你竟記得我的生日。）

⊃ 提議慶祝生日的說法一

M: Why don't we go celebrate for your birthday?
（我們何不一起去慶祝你的生日？）

W: That sounds great!
（那是個好主意。）

⊃ 提議慶祝生日的說法二

W: Do you have plans tonight for your birthday?
（你今晚過生日，有什麼計畫沒有？）

M: No, I don't.
（沒有。）

Do you have any suggestions?
（你有什麼建議嗎？）

每課一句 3秒鐘，強化英語力！

📢 How old are you now?
（你現在到底幾歲了？）

📢 Has anyone asked you to lunch yet?
（有人邀你吃午餐了嗎？）

📢 Let me buy you lunch.
（我來請你吃午餐吧。）

📢 Did the office get you a cake?
（辦公室裡有沒有為你買蛋糕？）

常用單字 3秒鐘，強化單字力！

flattered [ˈflætɚd]		感到受寵若驚
remember [rɪˈmɛmbɚ]		記得
lonely [ˈlonlɪ]		孤獨
celebrate [ˈsɛləbret]		慶祝
birthday cake		生日蛋糕

📢 A contented man is always rich.
（知足的人最富有。）

朋友結婚

I wish you all the best.
祝你幸福！

精華短句 一學就會！最簡單、迷你的會話

- Is this the big weekend?
  （本週末就是大日子了吧？）

- I need your blessing.
  （我需要你的祝福。）

- Where will the wedding be at?
  （婚禮在哪兒舉行呀？）

- It will be a hectic week for you!
  （這星期你準得要很忙！）

- No kidding!
  （就是呀！）

- How was the wedding?
  （婚禮一切順利吧？）

實況會話 靈活運用！會話、聽力同步加強

外：	So, is this the big weekend?	那麼，這個週末就是大日子了？
中：	Yes, it is.	是的。
外：	Where will the wedding be at?	婚禮在哪裡舉行？
中：	Our local church.	我們的本地教會。
外：	That is great. I wish you all the best.	那好極了。 祝你幸福！
中：	Thank you. I need your blessing.	謝謝。 我需要你的祝福。
外：	It will be a hectic week for you!	這星期你肯定要忙成一團。
中：	No kidding!	就是呀！

⊃ 向結婚人道喜，怎麼說？

M: Congratulations on your wedding.
（恭禧你結婚。）

W: Thank you.
（謝謝。）

⊃ 朋友的女兒結婚過後

M: How was the wedding going?
（婚禮進行得如何？）

W: It went well, but I am sad to have my daughter gone.
（一切都好，只是女兒嫁走了，我有些傷心。）

⊃ 自願幫忙打點結婚雜務，怎麼說？

M: Do you need any help getting last minute things together for the wedding?
（需不需要幫忙打點婚禮雜七雜八的事情？）

W: No, but I really appreciate the offer.
（不用，但我真的很感激你的提議。）

🔊 Bashfulness is an enemy to poverty.
（害羞是財富的敵人。）

每課一句 *3秒鐘，強化英語力！*

🔊 I wish you all the happiness in life.
（祝你一生幸福。）

🔊 I am sure it was a beautiful wedding.
（我可以肯定那一定是個很美的婚禮。）

🔊 I hope you did not have any big problems with the wedding.
（我希望你的婚禮一切順利。）

常用單字 *3秒鐘，強化單字力！*

wedding ['wɛdɪŋ]	婚禮；結婚
church [tʃɝtʃ]	教堂
hectic ['hɛktɪk]	忙成一團
congratulations [kən,grætʃə'leʃənz]	恭禧
last minute things	最後雜事
get ~ together	打點～

英語系列：26

跟老外交友學英語

作者／施孝昌
出版者／哈福企業有限公司
地址／新北市中和區景新街 347 號 11 樓之 6
電話／(02) 2945-6285　傳真／(02) 2945-6986
郵政劃撥／31598840　戶名／哈福企業有限公司
出版日期／2016 年 3 月
定價／NT$ 299 元（附 MP3）

全球華文國際市場總代理／采舍國際有限公司
地址／新北市中和區中山路 2 段 366 巷 10 號 3 樓
電話／(02) 8245-8786　傳真／(02) 8245-8718
網址／www.silkbook.com　新絲路華文網

香港澳門總經銷／和平圖書有限公司
地址／香港柴灣嘉業街 12 號百樂門大廈 17 樓
電話／(852) 2804-6687　傳真／(852) 2804-6409
定價／港幣 100 元（附 MP3）

視覺設計／Wan Wan
內文排版／Jo Jo
email／haanet68@Gmail.com

郵撥打九折，郵撥未滿 500 元，酌收 1 成運費，
滿 500 元以上者免運費

國家圖書館出版品預行編目資料

跟老外交友學英語 / 施孝昌◎著 -- 新北市：哈福企業，
2016.03
　面；　公分. -（英語系列；25）
ISBN 978-986-5616-50-2(平裝附光碟片)

1.英語 2.會話

805.188　　　　　　　　　　　　105002600

哈福

哈福